THE BIRCHBARK HOUSE

ALSO BY LOUISE ERDRICH:

Grandmother's Pigeon
Illustrated by Jim LaMarche

THE BIRCHBARK HOUSE

Louise Erdrich

with illustrations by the author

Disney • HYPERION

LOS ANGELES   NEW YORK

Designed by Christine Kettner

First Hardcover Edition, July 1999

First Paperback Edition, June 2002

23

Printed in the United States of America

LIBRARY OF CONGRESS CATALOGING-IN-PUBLICATION DATA

Erdrich, Louise.

The birchbark house/by Louise Erdrich.—1st ed.

p. cm.

Summary: Omakayas, a seven-year-old Native American girl of the Ojibwa tribe, lives through
the joys of summer and the perils of winter on an island in Lake Superior in 1847.

1. Ojibwa Indians—Juvenile fiction. [1. Ojiwba Indians—Fiction.
2. Indians of North America—Fiction. 3. Islands—Fiction. 4. Seasons—Fiction.] I. Title.

ISBN 0-7868-0300-2 (trade)—ISBN 0-7868-2241-4 (lib.)

ISBN 0-7868-1454-3 (pbk.)

PZ7.E72554Bi 1999   [Fic]—dc21 98-46366

Visit www.DisneyBooks.com

FAC-025438-16181

SUSTAINABLE FORESTRY INITIATIVE

Certified Chain of Custody
Promoting Sustainable Forestry

www.sfiprogram.org
SFI-01054

The SFI label applies to the text stock

To Persia,

whose song heals

THANKS AND ACKNOWLEDGMENTS

My mother, Rita Gourneau Erdrich, and my sister Lise Erdrich, researched our family life and found ancestors on both sides who lived on Madeline Island during the time in which this book is set. One of them was Gatay Manomin, or Old Wild Rice. I'd like to thank him and all of his descendants, my extended family.

The name Omakayas appears on a Turtle Mountain census. I am using it in the original translation because I've been told those old names should be given life. The name is pronounced Oh-MAH-kay-ahs. The more accepted spelling and pronunciation of this name is Omakakeyens (Oh-MAH-kah-KEY-aynz); however, I decided to remain true to the name as it was pronounced and spelled in 1892. Dear reader, when you speak this name out loud you will be honoring the life of an Ojibwa girl who lived long ago.

This book and those that will follow are an attempt to retrace my own family's history. Special thanks to Steve and Mary Cotherman, and all of the devoted people at the Madeline Island Historical Society. Mom and sister Angie, thanks for your constant encouragement with the illustrations. I would especially like to thank my daughter, Persia, who read this book when it was a manuscript and made important suggestions. Apijigo megwetch, Winona LaDuke. You started me thinking. All of my Ojibwa teachers, Naawigiizis (Jim Clark), Jesse Clark, Dennis Jones and Lorraine Jones, Keller Paap, and Lisa LaRonge, apijigo megwetch. All mistakes are mine.

CONTENTS

Contents

THE BIRCHBARK HOUSE

THE GIRL FROM
SPIRIT ISLAND

HE ONLY PERSON LEFT ALIVE on the island was a baby girl. The tired men who had come there to pick up furs from the Anishinabe people stood uneasily on the rocky shore. The voyageurs watched from a distance as the baby crawled in a circle, whimpering and pitiful. Her tiny dress of good blue wool was embroidered with white beads and ribbons, and her new makazins were carefully sewn. It was clear she had been loved. It was also clear that the family who had loved her was gone. All of the fires in the village were cold. The dead lay sadly in blankets, curled as as though sleeping. Smallpox had killed them all.

The voyageurs trembled at the thought that the disease might already have chosen one of them. Surely, they muttered, the baby had the sickness, too. *She's sick. She looks tired*, said one man when she lay down against one of the blanketed figures. *Let her sleep*. Birds were singing, dozens of tiny white-throated sparrows. The trilling, rippling sweetness of their songs contrasted strangely with the silent horror below. First one then the other of the men turned away. They got back into their canoes.

As they paddled toward the next island, all were silent, thoughtful. Some wore hard expressions. One man had tears in his eyes. His name was Hat; he thought of his wife and decided he would tell her about the baby. If there was anyone in the world who'd go and rescue that little girl, it was his wife. He shivered a little as he thought of her. He couldn't help it. Tallow, she was called, and sometimes she scared him with her temper. Other times, he was amazed at her courage. He grimaced in shame—unlike him, his wife was afraid of nothing.

Neebin

(SUMMER)

CHAPTER ONE

The Birchbark House

 HE WAS NAMED OMAKAYAS, or Little Frog, because her first step was a hop. She grew into a nimble young girl of seven winters, a thoughtful girl with shining brown eyes and a wide grin, only missing her two top front teeth. She touched her upper lip. She still wasn't used to those teeth gone, and was impatient for new, grown-up teeth to complete her smile. Just like her namesake, Omakayas now stared long at the silky patch of bog before she gathered herself and jumped. One hummock. Safety. Omakayas sprang wide again. This time she landed on the very tip-top of a pointed old stump. She balanced there, looking all around. The lagoon water moved in sparkling crescents.

Thick swales of swamp grass rippled. Mud turtles napped in the sun. The world was so calm that Omakayas could hear herself blink. Only the sweet call of a solitary white-throated sparrow pierced the cool of the woods beyond.

All of a sudden Grandma yelled.

"I found it!"

Startled, Omakayas slipped and spun her arms in wheels. She teetered, but somehow kept her balance. Two big, skipping hops, another leap, and she was on dry land. She stepped over spongy leaves and moss, into the woods where the sparrows sang nesting songs in delicate relays.

"Where are you?" Nokomis yelled again. "I found the tree!"

"I'm coming," Omakayas called back to her grandmother.

It was spring, time to cut the birchbark.

◄o►

All winter long Omakayas's family lived in a cabin of sweet-scented cedar at the edge of the village of La-Pointe, on an island in Lake Superior that her people called Moningwanaykaning, Island of the Golden-Breasted Woodpecker. As soon as the earth warmed, the birchbark house always took shape under Nokomis's swift hands. Now the dappled light of tiny new leaves moved on Grandma's beautiful, softly lined face. In one hand she waved her sharp knife, taken from the beaded pouch on her hip. In the other hand she held tobacco. Nokomis was ready to make an offering to the spirits, or manitous. They loved tobacco. Omakayas banged the tree her grandmother had found.

"Yes, here, here it is! This one!"

Omakayas was skinny, wiry, and tough for seven winters. She slammed the trunk of the birch with a big rotten stick. Splinters of soft wood flew.

"Booni!" Nokomis scolded. "Leave it alone!"

She walked up to the tree and put her leathery paw-like hands on the smooth bark, feeling for flaws. "Yes," she decided, her eyes sparkling at her granddaughter. "A good one."

"Is it ready?"

"Geget," said Nokomis. "Surely."

Nokomis's tobacco pouch was decorated with blue and white beads in the shape of a pipe. She had owned this tobacco bag ever since Omakayas could remember. When she talked to the manitous, Nokomis dipped out a pinch of tobacco.

"Old Sister," she said to the birchbark tree, "we need your skin for our shelter."

At the base of the tree, Nokomis left her offering, sweet and fragrant. Then she peered closely, deciding just where to make the first cut. Suddenly, she pressed her razor-sharp knife into the bark. Omakayas stepped back. Light filtered golden and green onto their faces. Tiny white flowers poked out of dead leaves. There were still traces of grainy old snowbanks in the shadiest spots, but in places the sun was actually hot. *Pow!* As soon as Grandma made the proper cuts, the birchbark, filled with spring water, nearly burst from the tree!

Omakayas helped her grandmother carefully push the bark aside, then the two peeled it away strip by strip. She and Omakayas carried the light papery pink-brown rolls out of the woods, down a trail to a special place near the water.

Here, they set up the birchbark house.

Damp ground made Nokomis's old bones ache, so she spread out her brown cattail mat and sat down there to sew those pieces of bark together. Omakayas helped her, threading the tough basswood strands through holes punched by Grandma's awl. Meanwhile, Mama and Omakayas's older sister tied together a frame of bent willow poles. Finally, as the light faded, they fastened the mats of bark onto the willow frame, a half skeleton of pliable saplings. The bark mats overlapped like shingles, to shed the rain. Each one was secured to the next, so as not to blow off in a storm. When the house was swept out, smoothed, fussily arranged, and admired, they moved in. The children—Omakayas's brother Little Pinch, baby Neewo, Omakayas's older sister, pretty Angeline, and Omakayas herself—spread their blankets around the stone fire pit. Mama and Nokomis hung the smoky woven bags of rice and tools and medicines from the willow poles above.

Omakayas's family were Anishinabeg and this was their island. Her father, her Deydey, was in the fur trade business, which meant that he was often gone, paddling the great canoes for the fur company or sometimes trapping animals himself. Yellow Kettle, her mother, was quick-tempered but always laughing, and her eyes shrewdly took in the world. Yellow Kettle was a strong-looking woman, and beautiful. Her smile was generous, enigmatic, slightly crooked, and kind. She missed nothing when it came to her children—it was impossible to hide a half-done job, ridiculous even to think of sneaking away in the morning before gathering wood for the fire and water for her cooking pot. And if Mama didn't notice the younger children's whereabouts, Omakayas's older sister, Angeline, surely would.

Angeline was smart and so pretty people turned in their tracks to stare at her. Her hair was thick, her hands clever. The beads in her designs were laid down in strict rows. Her stitches never faltered. Her steps, when she walked or danced, were clear and graceful. She was so perfect that Omakayas despaired. Still, she hoped that she herself would turn out like Angeline, and was sometimes embarrassed to find herself following at Angeline's heels like a puppy. Most of the time Angeline was kind to Omakayas, and let her tag along and admire, from a distance. But there were also times her words were sharp as bee stings, and at those times Omakayas shed tears her sister never knew or probably even cared about, for as very beautiful people sometimes are, Angeline could be just a little coldhearted at times.

Omakayas's little brother Pinch was the only really big problem in her life. The sad truth was, and she couldn't tell this to a single person, Omakayas didn't like Little Pinch. She thought there was something wrong with him—so greedy, so loud! But although his ways were mischievous and bold, Pinch loved his mother deeply, and he clung to her side. In fact, he took up all her attention, even more than the baby! He clutched Mama's skirts with fat, tough little fingers. He yelled at Omakayas if she was slow in giving up her willow doll, her little rock people, or anything else for that matter, including food, special pieces of driftwood she found, even her favorite sleeping place, near Grandma. He thought he deserved *everything*.

At least when it came to Neewo there was nothing to complain about. He was so sweet that Omakayas often pretended that he was her very own baby. Of course, she hardly ever got to hold him, for he was still very young. Still, she was sure he preferred her to Angeline, and certainly to Pinch. Sometimes he even held his arms out to her when Mama was holding him, and yelled with delight when Omakayas picked him up.

◄○►

As it grew dark, the family ate makuks of moose stew and fresh greens and berries, licked their fingers and bowls clean, and at last rolled themselves into warm, fluffy rabbit-skin blankets that still smelled of the cedary smoke of their winter cabin. They were glad to be close to fire, sleeping on soft grassy earth, under leafy sky, and best of all, near water. They fell asleep to the peaceful, curious, continual lapping sound of waves. The fresh wind across the big lake blew away the smoke of cooking fires and vanquished the mosquitoes that came out in whining droves and had plagued them in town. It was good to sleep where the village dogs didn't bark all night and where the only sound to disturb their dreams was the pine trees sifting wind in a lulling roar.

Unless, of course, it stormed.

The moon went down to a fingernail's sliver and the corn popped from the ground. The leaves of the birch grew big enough to flutter in the wind. And then, one night, the first storm of the summer struck the island and startled everybody from their dreams.

The fire was down to red winking eyes when Omakayas woke with an uneasy feeling. Something approached. She'd felt a footstep. Omakayas was always the one to sleep near Grandma and now she rolled close. There was a lonely insistence to the sound of the wind, and then everything went still. Far off, she heard one huge footstep. There was a long silence. Then another step fell. The earth shook slightly beneath her, vibrated as though she lay on the head of a vast drum.

A drum! She remembered that Grandma had said the island was the drum of the thunder beings. Closer and closer they came, shaking earth with their footsteps. Omakayas's lonely feeling became fright. She hid her face and tried not to think of balls of witch fire or the hooting of Grandfather Owl. She tried to keep herself from picturing pakuks, the skeletons of little children, flying through the woods, or the icy breath of giant windigos striding over the ground, cracking trees off with every foot crunch. Another step. Another and another fell and then the wind howled to life. Rain slashed against the tightly sewn walls. A breath of air stirred up the slumbering coals and cast shadows leaping and fighting on the inside walls of the little birchbark house.

The willow poles trembled, bouncing with the force of the gusts of wind. The birchbark scraped and flapped but was held on with tight stitches. Omakayas hid her face as thunder rolled, smacking onto the lakeshore, waking everything and everyone with its quick violence. The storm punished the ground and then passed over, dying off in softer mumbles. The dull thuds of thunder falling in the distance now felt comforting, and before the sounds entirely faded, Omakayas was asleep.

◄◦►

Moningwanaykaning, Island of the Golden-Breasted Woodpecker, sparkled innocently after that night of raw thunder and lightning. Omakayas woke and immediately began wondering. What had the storm done to the trees? What had the waves washed onto the beach? What interesting bits of wood that she could use for pretend dolls? What kind of day would it be? Were the little berries on the edge of the path ripe yet? An unpleasant piece of wondering came to her, too. Had her mother finished scraping and tanning that ugly moose hide or would she have to help her? Oh, she hoped not. How she hoped! There was a saying she hated. Grandma said it all too often. "Each animal," she would say, "has just enough brains to tan its own hide." Mama tanned the moose hide with the very brains of the moose and Omakayas hated the oozy feel of them on her hands, not to mention the boring, endless scraping and rubbing that went into making a hide soft enough for makazins.

From a fire in the center of the bark house a thin curl of smoke rose, then vanished through a crescent of sunlight in the roof. If only she could escape with the smoke! She could already hear Mama and Grandma outside at the cooking fires. They were planning the day's work. In no time at all, that soaking moose hide would be stretched on a branch frame and she would be required to scrape at it with the sharpened deer's shoulder bone that her mother kept in a bundle of useful things near the door. Her arms would tire; they would feel like falling off. Her fingers would go numb. Her back would hurt. The awful smell would get into her skin. And meanwhile, all the little birds would find the luscious patch of berries she alone knew about. By the time she got that stupid old moose hide softened up, they would have eaten every last berry. She must act. Quickly!

The air was fresh, delicious, smelling of new leaves in the woods, just-popped-out mushrooms, the pelts of young deer. The air flowed in, rainwashed, under the strips of birchbark walls she had helped sew together yesterday. Like a small, striped snake, like a salamander, or a squirrel maybe, or a raccoon, something quick, little, harmless, and desperate, she slid, crept, wiggled underneath the sides of the summer house. The seam of bark

THE BIRCHBARK HOUSE

caught her in the small of the back, stuck tight. If only
she hadn't done such a good job of sewing it up! If
only, too, Angeline didn't have such quick ears and sure
knowledge of her whereabouts at all times. There was
a firm pressure suddenly at the small of her back,
still caught on the inside. Her sister's foot. Her sister's
gloating voice.

"Neshemay! Baby sister! Little Frog, don't go jumping off!"

Then there was her mother, rounding the back of
the house, one side of her hair still flowing down, un-
braided. She glanced in surprise at Omakayas, trapped,
and then unable to hide her amusement, a big grin
spread over Mama's face. Her admired big sister, her
beloved mother, laughing! There was Omakayas—laughter from the front and laughter from behind—and suddenly, all of last night's thunder in her heart.

◄o►

Omakayas sat near the cooking fire and slowly, with
deep inner fury, ate a bowl of cold stew. She dragged
out time waiting for her hateful job to start. Mama
was wrestling that hide out of the stream now, where it
had been soaking for days and nights, gathering up its
scummy, woolly slime. Mama had already set up the

dreaded frame of branches and there were strings of hide nearby that she would use to tie the skin up tight so that it could be worked. Omakayas knew how important it was to tan the skin, how her mother would cut up the soft smoked hide and sew on the winter's makazins all summer. She pictured her mother finishing them with lovely, soft toe puckers so the girls' feet could twitch and dance. She could imagine Yellow Kettle beading them, lining them inside with the silkiest rabbit fur and pieces of an old wool blanket. Yes, it was an important task, but Omakayas still didn't want it. She finished her stew, cleaned the bowl out with sand at the shore of the lake, and waited with a sigh for her mother to ask her to fetch the deer-bone scraper.

Her mother said something else, though.

"I need my scissors!"

Omakayas sat up, suddenly full of energy.

Omakayas's mother was well known for owning a pair of scissors, and other women were always borrowing them. Omakayas's first job ever since she could walk was to fetch her mother's scissors, kept safe from her small fingers in a beaded woolen case, and bring them home. She had never failed, for it was a job she liked not only because she was sometimes given a handful of manomin, rice, or a little chunk of maple sugar by the borrowing lady, but because there were things to see on the way there and back.

Right now her sister, Angeline, was digging at the ground near spruce trees and cutting lengths of the roots, used to secure the house better and to finish baskets. She was cheerful, humming at her work, glad to have gotten the better of Omakayas. She'd show Angeline! Let her work until her hands fell off! Omakayas had a fun job to do!

"Go fetch me the scissors from Old Tallow," said Omakayas's mother. Without a moment's hesitation, before Mama changed her mind and remembered about the help she needed with the stinky hide, Omakayas ran off.

CHAPTER TWO

Old Tallow

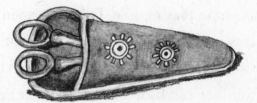

 LTHOUGH SHE LIVED in town, Old Tallow was so isolated by the force and strangeness of her personality that she could have been surrounded by a huge dark forest. She had never had any children, and each of her three husbands had slunk off in turn during the night, never to be seen again. Nobody knew exactly what it was that Tallow, in her younger days, had done to drive them off. It had probably been something terrible. After the last husband left, her face seemed to have gotten old suddenly, though the rest of her hadn't weakened. She was a rangy woman over six feet in height. She was powerful, lean, and lived surrounded by ferocious animals more wolf than dog and fiercely devoted to her. Old Tallow could bring down a bear with her pack of dogs, her gun, or even the razor-sharp spear that she practiced throwing into the splintered base of a tree. The dogs were bull-tough and the yellow one, particularly, showed its wolf origins in the springy length of its legs.

For some reason, Old Tallow seemed to treat her, Omakayas, somewhat differently than other children. She didn't scream at her, or heap distain on her, order her away from her cabin or set her dogs on her. Omakayas thought perhaps it was because Old Tallow respected her mama and grandma. Old Tallow respected almost nobody else, so this was extra-meaningful. The three women often sat together, talking in the dusk. Also, Old Tallow, who loved to hunt and was very skilled, shared her catch with them when Deydey was gone. They would sometimes wake to find a haunch of venison just inside the door, or bear meat, a fish or two. In fact, she now remembered that Old Tallow was responsible for the hide of the moose, which she had shared. Old Tallow liked to make her deliveries at night, which was another thing. Most other people hated to go about in the dark when Grandfather Owl was calling *kokoko, kokoko,* and anything could happen.

But of course, Old Tallow was afraid of nothing.

Omakayas approached Tallow's cabin warily because of the dogs. She stood for a moment at the end of the trail, gathering her confidence before she rounded the corner. One dog in particular seemed to hate her—the big yellow one. Omakayas was careful not to startle him or gaze too long into his mean, clouded eyes. Once, he had snapped at her and worried the sleeve of her dress. There he stood now, to bar her way to Tallow's door. Omakayas screwed up her courage, breathed calmly. She walked forward, shoving him aside as though she had not a care for his dripping teeth. She got ready to deliver a hard kick if he lunged, and walked past him without showing her fear. The dog bristled at her, baring its teeth in an ugly snarl, but let her pass by. The other dogs—the black, the brown with the lopped-off tail, the small whitish one, and the droopy orange runt—merely looked alert and regarded her with neutral interest.

Old Tallow's cabin was small, neat, thickly mudded between logs. There was a log bench beside the door. Sure enough, Old Tallow sat upon it smoking her pipe. A fragrant curl of sweet kinnikinnick smoke stirred from the red stone bowl.

As though she had known Omakayas was coming for the precious scissors, Old Tallow had them on her lap, safe in the bead-decorated pouch of red trade wool that Mama had made specially to hold them.

"Ahneen, little skinny one," she growled.

Old Tallow's legs stuck out like poles, tattered makazins flapped on her wagging feet as she drew impatiently upon her pipe. She tamped the bowl of the pipe with huge hands; her arms were long and sinewy. The old blue dress she wore was trimmed with the teeth of fox at the collar, beaded halfway around the scraggly, ripped hem. Tallow, in her galloping hunts through the woods, was hard on clothes and wore out her makazins one pair right after the next. Even now, a toe stuck out from the ripped front seam. She tucked her braids up underneath a man's hat, a white man's hat with a heavy brim. She was hardly seen without it, even in her own house. In the band of the hat she always wore a little gold-shafted feather. This was the feather of the golden-breasted woodpecker, the bird that gave its name and chattering cry to this island.

"You want the scissors!" Her voice was abrupt, but not unkind.

"Yes," said Omakayas, glad that Old Tallow was outside. The yellow dog knew it was wrong to intimidate Omakayas. Sure enough, Old Tallow scolded him.

"You," she shrieked at the snarling dog, "booni!

Leave her alone. This is your last warning! Touch her and you die!"

The yellow dog turned aside, shrugging and cringing mean-spiritedly, eyeing Omakayas. She imagined she heard the yellow dog say, *I'll get you next time! Wait until there's just the two of us. You'll see!*

Relieved, Omakayas walked past the other dogs straight up to the old woman and stood before her.

"Ahneen, my auntie," she said. "Mino aya sana."

She wished the old woman good health, and called her "Auntie" because it was a sign of affection, though Omakayas was really not sure exactly what she felt. After she'd spoken, she stood politely, waiting. Old Tallow smiled, nodded, and blew a blast of smoke out her nostrils. Then she put her hand into the pouch at her waist. She rummaged around for a bit, then suddenly drew forth a small, grime-covered lump of maple sugar, rock-hard and wonderful.

"You take this," she said, her voice cracked and dry, as though salted. "And this, too." She handed Omakayas the scissors, waved her back onto the trail, and as this was as friendly as Old Tallow ever got, Omakayas went away satisfied.

-<o>-

Before she went back on the trail, Omakayas rinsed off the old candy lump in the lake. It came out beautifully, creamy-golden, translucent and grainy-dark. And sweet. She started walking, her treasure now wrapped in a leaf. As she walked, Omakayas thought. There was no way to share such a tough nut of sweetness. How would she divide it? Omakayas decided she did not want to cause trouble at home. Furthermore, it suddenly made sense to her that at least one person in the family should get the full effect of the maple sugar. She would pop the whole thing into her mouth. All at once! This would save problems. Aaaaah. The lump was delicious, tasting of spring sweetness and the inside of trees. Besides, Omakayas reasoned, as she walked contentedly along, the taste of the sugar would save her from eating every one of the berries she was sure she would find on the path.

Omakayas's feet moved slower and even slower yet. For one thing, the moose hide waited. For another, she was still angry with her older sister, and didn't want to see Angeline. She could still feel that sister foot pressing hateful on her back. If only there were some way to impress Angeline, cause her envy, make her say, "Can I have some of those berries, please, please, please?" You can be sure, Omakayas thought, her face taking on a faraway, haughty expression, she would be slow in answering! Yet the worst of it was this: her sister was usually on her side, helping her plan tricks on the other children in the village or gathering new ferns or snaring rabbits, visiting the grave houses looking for sugar or food left for the spirits, tossing off her clothes to swim with her. And to have her older sister laugh at her hurt Omakayas so much inside that she both wanted Angeline to smile in surprise, to be proud, to envy her, and to feel rotten and be sorry forever. So Omakayas took the slow way back looking for odaemin, little red heartberries, in the sunny margins of the woods near the ground.

She carefully removed the hard lump of sweetness from her mouth, stuck it back in its leaf just inside the pocket of her dress. Just as the taste of maple sugar faded along her tongue, she bent over, pushed back delicate leaves, and found masses of plump red little berries. Ah! One, two, three. She'd eaten a huge handful. Another. She grinned, thinking that she'd allow her sister to return with her to plunder them, but only if Angeline changed her ways.

All of a sudden, a rustle and then a thump in a bush ahead made Omakayas freeze. A long moment passed as she stared through the dark leaves. Suddenly, *crash!* Two bear cubs burst from the bush and rushed pell-mell, tumbling head over heels straight for her. They came on in such a hurry that they didn't see Omakayas until they were nearly in her lap, and then, with comical looks of shock, they tried to stop themselves. One flew flat on its face, bumping its nose and squealing. The other twisted in midair and landed in a heap on the ground, shaking its head in confusion at Omakayas.

The bear boys looked at her. Slowly, she put out

her open hand filled with heartberries. Curious, the cubs jumped forward, lost their nerve. They scampered backward, and then crept forward shyly again. The smaller cub seemed slightly bolder and sniffed at Omakayas's hand.

The bear cub took one berry, then jumped away in seeming fright at its own bold act. But the taste of the berry seemed to banish fear. The two now tumbled at her, growling, mock-ferocious. Their long pink tongues touched up every berry from her hands, eagerly flicking them from her fingers as fast as she could pick. They seemed to like the game. It could have gone on for hours, that is, until she stood upright. Then they tumbled backward in alarm. Their chubby bottoms rolled them over like playing balls, and she laughed out loud. She realized they had thought Omakayas was their own size. They were astonished the same way Omakayas had been the first time she saw the trader unfold a seeing glass, something he called a telescope, a long, shiny tube that grew in his hands.

She bent down again.

"Ahneen, little brothers," she said to them kindly, and they came forward.

She looked around. No mother bear. Omakayas was well aware that she shouldn't stay so close to these cubs, but after all, they seemed deserted. She looked around again. They were orphans! Perhaps the mother bear's skin was now draped across Old Tallow's bed, although she hadn't heard about a recent kill. But still, no mother bear in sight. And these little ones so hungry. Wouldn't her big sister be thrilled when Omakayas returned with these two new brothers! Eagerly, Omakayas began to plan out her triumphant walk back to the house. She would enter the little clearing with the cubs, one at her heels and one before her. Everyone would make way, impressed. She would lead the bear cubs around the fire four times before she presented one of them to Angeline, who would look at her with new respect.

◄o►

There was no warning. One moment Omakayas was wiggling a leafy stick, making it move on the ground so the cubs would jump on it, biting fiercely. The next moment, she found herself flipped over on her back and pinned underneath a huge, powerful, heavy thing that sent down a horrible stink. It was the sow bear, the mother. Breathing on her a stale breath of decayed old deer-hides and skunk cabbages and dead mushrooms. Owah! The surprising thing was, Omakayas realized later, that although she had no memory of doing so, she had the scissors out of their case and open, the sharp ends pointing at the bear's heart. But she didn't use them as a knife. She knew for certain that *she should not move.* If the bear began to bite and claw, she would have to plunge the tip of the scissors straight in between the bear's strong ribs, use all of her strength, sink the blade all the way in to the rounded hilt and then jump clear, if she could, while the bear went through its death agony. If she couldn't get clear, Omakayas knew she would have to roll up in a ball and endure the bear's fury. She would probably be clawed from head to foot, bitten to pieces, scattered all over the ground.

Until the mother bear made the first move,

Omakayas knew she should stay still, or as still as possible, given the terrified jumping of her heart.

For long moments, the bear tested her with every sense, staring down with her weak eyes, listening, and most of all smelling her. The bear smelled the morning's moose meat stew Omakayas had eaten, the wild onion seasoning and the dusty bit of maple sugar from Old Tallow stuck to the inside of her pocket. How she hoped the bear did not smell the bear-killing dogs or the bear claw that swung on a silver hoop from Old Tallow's earlobe. Perhaps the bear smelled the kind touch of Grandma and Mama's bone-and-sprucewood comb, her baby brother's cuddling body, the skins and mats she had slept in, and Little Pinch, who had whined and sobbed

the night before. The bear smelled on Omakayas's skin the smell of its own cousin's bear grease used to ward off mosquitoes. Fish from the night before last night. The berries she was eating. The bear smelled all.

Omakayas couldn't help but smell her back. Bears eat anything and this one had just eaten something ancient and foul. Hiyn! Omakayas took shallow breaths. Perhaps it was to take her mind off the scent of dead things on the bear's breath that she accidentally closed the scissors, shearing off a tiny clip of bear fur, and then to cover her horror at this mistake, started to talk.

"Nokomis," she said to the bear, calling her grandmother. "I didn't mean any harm. I was only playing with your children. Gaween onjidah. Please forgive me."

The bear cuffed at Omakayas, but in a warning manner, not savagely, to hurt. Then the bear leaned back, nose working, as though she could scent the meaning of the human words. Encouraged, Omakayas continued.

"I fed them some berries. I wanted to bring them home, to adopt them, have them live with me at my house as my little brothers. But now that you're here, Grandmother, I will leave quietly. These scissors in my hands are not for killing, just for sewing. They are nothing compared to your teeth and claws."

And indeed, Omakayas's voice trembled slightly as

the bear made a gurgling sound deep in her throat and bared her long, curved yellowish teeth, so good at ripping and tearing. But having totaled up all of the smells and sifted them for information, the bear seemed to have decided that Omakayas was no threat. She sat back on her haunches like a huge dog. Swinging her head around, she gave a short, quick slap at one of the cubs that sent it reeling away from Omakayas. It was as though she were telling them they had done wrong to approach this human animal, and should now stay away from her. Omakayas's heart squeezed painfully. Even though it was clear her life was to be spared, she felt the loss of her new brothers.

"I wouldn't ever hurt them," she said again.

The little cubs piled against their mother, clung to her. For a long moment the great bear sat calmly with them, deciding where to go. Then, in no hurry, they rose in one piece of dark fur. One bear boy broke away, again tried to get near Oma- kayas. The other looked longingly at her, but the big bear mother abruptly nosed them down the trail.

CHAPTER THREE

The Return

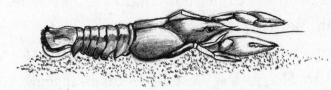

 FTER SHE RETURNED with the scissors, Omakayas quietly took up the deer bone from her mother's skin bag and began working on the moose hide without being asked. Her mother looked at her in some surprise, but said nothing. Angeline said that she had meant to do the work, but Omakayas merely shook her head.

"Go for a swim," she told her sister. "See what the waves brought to the shore last night. Catch some crayfish, ashaageshinh, watch out for their claws. I don't mind helping."

Angeline and Mama looked at Omakayas as though

they couldn't have heard right. But when Omakayas nodded to signal that she meant what she said, and Mama nodded, Angeline started with delight. She had to do grown-up work now every day, and she rarely had free time to play. Angeline looked hopefully at her mother, who waved her out toward the lakeshore. Off she ran, skipping and bounding in her thin summer makazins, her soft old tradecloth dress fluttering.

Baby Neewo was sleeping in his tikinagun. Little brother Pinch was killing his willow doll men over and over with a rock. Omakayas concentrated now on the work beneath her hands. She needed to think about what had just happened to her. Boring work was just what she wanted. Her mind could wander. She sighed, irritated by the smell and buzzing flies. At least there was some breeze that day to blow away the smell. While scraping the hide, she let her thoughts roam.

The longer she thought about her encounter with the mother bear, the more Omakayas was convinced that something she did not understand had passed between the two of them. Not words. Perhaps they had communicated in smells. Or maybe in a language of feelings. Her terror, the bear's pity. Perhaps it was her own grandmother's advice that had saved her life. Nokomis had told her that the bear must be addressed with the greatest respect, as a treasured relative, that the bear had human qualities and nobody quite understood the bear. But that bears understood humans quite well.

When a bear was killed and its skin was off, Omakayas knew it looked fearfully like a person. She'd also heard that bears laugh and cry, just as humans do. Grandma had once seen a bear rocking its young in her arms just as a human mother rocks its young. Nobody on the island ever tossed the bones of a bear aside. Every bear bone was gathered respectfully and buried, all together. At a bear feast, the bear's skull was ribboned and set out on a good red cloth, spoken to, honored.

Yes, there was something about what had happened that made Omakayas very quiet. As she scraped at the hide, nicking bits of meat and gristle from the surface, she began to get all empty and peculiar and faint inside. A thought was coming. A voice approached. This happened to her sometimes. A dizzy feeling would pass over her. If she attended to it closely, once it was gone she would know something a little extra, as though she'd overheard two spirits talking.

She kept scraping, gritting her teeth, and held on to her thoughts, for once again she could feel the presence of the powerful mother bear at her shoulder. Although there were no words and although there was no odor of her presence, no bear sounds, no tracks, Omakayas's heart lightened. Turning from her work, she knew the bear had visited her. She knew the bear had followed her home. She knew that when she needed the bear she would be able to call on the bear. The bear had understood something she had said and she had understood something the bear had thought, and although she couldn't tell exactly what, Omakayas turned back to her task with her head clear and her hands cheerful.

She worked so hard, all through that afternoon, that her grandma, watching her keenly, made a great fuss over the work Omakayas had done on the hide. She said

Omakayas had done as well as a full-grown woman. Her mother promised her a very special pair of winter makazins and Angeline even braided her hair with one of her own red ribbons.

<o>

Neewo means "fourth" and that was what they called the baby, but soon, Grandma said, the baby would have to have a name. The tiny boy was a spirit, so far, who had come to live here and was deciding whether or not to stay. Grandma told Omakayas to be careful with him, little baby Neewo, because he might decide to go back to the other place if he thought his big sister was mean. So Omakayas was very gentle with the baby. She rocked him in the branch-held tikinagun with great consideration. She gathered spongy moss and old oak punk to stuff into the cradle board and use as a diaper. She twirled and dangled the little web of sinew and the tobacco ties and bitten birchbark pretties that Grandma tied onto the head guard of the tikinagun. She fed Neewo tiny bits of the best food when Mama wasn't looking. She felt, in her heart, streams of love for the baby pouring through and she begged her mother to let her take Neewo out and cart him to the lake on her hip.

But her mother smiled and touched Omakayas's

hair gently and shook her head. Gaween. No. She was too young. Grandma gave her the willow doll instead, told her to let the baby sleep, directed her to play with Little Pinch. But she knew what that would mean! Pinch would jump on her back and yell, "N'dai, get moving!" He would pull her braids. He would use her as a practice bow and arrow target. He would tip over the rock children and rock people she made of specially piled lake pebbles. He would destroy her rock people village down by the beach. No, she didn't want to play with him! Little Pinch? Never!

◄○►

Half the summer went by quickly after the visit from the bear. Omakayas stayed thoughtful. She helped hoe the corn patch almost every day, and never complained. She was kind, hardworking, patient. But she was also lost in her own thoughts. She startled when spoken to, went to sleep early and slept long, dreamed hard but couldn't remember the night's adventures. And she also had those dizzy moments that, her grandma said, meant she was special to the spirits. One day, her mother said to her grandmother, "If she wasn't so young, I'd give her the charcoal."

Grandma's deep and far-seeing eyes took in Omakayas. She seemed to see her granddaughter from the inside out. She watched Omakayas for a long time, then shook her head. No. Not yet. When a mother put charcoal on her child's face, it was a sign that the child was ready to starve for a vision, for power. A child with a blackened face didn't eat for days, and sometimes lived out in the woods alone until the spirits took pity on him or her and helped out with a special vision, a special visit, some information. But Omakayas was too young, according to Grandma, so Mama stirred the fire and worried. She had a lot to think about anyway, including a name for Baby Neewo, who was getting restless, trying to crawl out of the cradle board, acting as though he were anxious to have that name.

There were seven or eight people on the island who possessed the right to give names. Auntie Muskrat was one. Day Thunder, Swan, Old Man Migwans, and an ancient lady named Waubanikway knew how to dream names. Mama had asked, and each of them had tried. But not one of them had yet dreamed about a name for Neewo.

"For some reason," said Auntie Muskrat, "that

dream won't come." She even slept and fasted in the woods for a name, but the spirits were stubborn.

Old Waubanikway, who dreamed many names, had no name for the baby either, but she said that she would give no other name until she found one for the boy. She searched her dreams. Meantime, Baby Neewo grew! Omakayas decided in secret that the naming was up to her. In play, when just the two of them were together, she gave her little brother names. Bird names. Chick-adee, she called him. Apitchi. Robin. Little Junco. Sparrow. Grouse Chick. He seemed to like all of his bird names and when he heard them he grinned and waved his chubby arms in delight.

◄◦►

Omakayas could hardly resist Neewo, and played with him as often as she was allowed. There was something about the way he looked at her so sadly with big, soft eyes that made her want to cuddle him tight in her arms. There was something about the way he smiled when she made a face, surprised, so grateful, that made her kiss and touch his hair with great passion and indignation in her heart. He should have a name! And clearly, he wanted out of his tikinagun.

Omakayas wanted to help him to freedom.

Her chance came. One morning later on in the summer, Omakayas's mother, sister, grandma, and Little Pinch all wanted to go into the village and see the big canoes that had arrived to unload furs at the trader's. Omakayas's father, Mikwam, wasn't with these voyageurs, but Mama hoped that they might have news of him. The thought itself made Mama so anxious that she got ready to go off in haste, though Baby Neewo was still sleeping.

"Why don't you leave Neewo with me," Omakayas asked at the last moment. "I don't want to go. I can take care of him! You'll get there faster!"

She saw Mama's thoughts falter.

"You don't want to go?"

"I don't!"

Angeline and Grandma were already halfway down the path. Little Pinch was tugging on Mama's legging, whining for something to eat.

"All right," Mama decided. "We'll be right back. Now don't do anything. Just rock him, Omakayas, and play with him if he wakes up. Don't *do* anything!"

"Of course not," said Omakayas, trying hard not to show how excited she was to have her baby brother, Neewo, all to herself. She made herself tall and acted as grown-up as possible. Rocked him with one hand, gently, while she waved good-bye to Mama, and kept rocking long after her mother rounded the corner and disappeared into the ferny forest growth. He didn't wake. She quit rocking, just stared at his slumbering face. His lashes were so long and stiff, his little chin so chubby she wanted to stroke it, the skin on his cheeks so fine and delicate and soft she could hardly keep from brushing her lips across them. Tufts of silken hair stood out all over his head and his breath was still sweet with milk.

She touched him, very gently. Baby Neewo. Chickadee. The name popped into her mind. "Today, I'll call you Chickadee," she said.

His eyes opened, as though he understood. His look was bright and filled with secret jokes. He gazed up into her face. For a long time they looked at one another. It was perfect. It was love. And then his face crumpled, one fat tear squeezed from his eye, his lower lip shook. Suddenly, his mouth flew open and he bawled. Omakayas was so close, so dreamy and happy, that the force of it nearly flipped her back head over heels. His squall was like a whirlwind, like a sudden wash of freezing spray, like a harsh wind, weather like a hot wall of sound.

"Shuh, shuh, shuh . . . " Omakayas rocked and muttered, shushed, hummed, and sang an old lullaby her mother used. Nothing worked. Baby Neewo screamed louder, with increasing force. Omakayas was alarmed. She'd never heard him scream like this, had she? What was wrong? Was something—a biting fly, spider, tick, bee—something stinging or biting him inside the tight binding of his tikinagun? Only one way to find out— unbind him—and that was forbidden. Still, as Neewo's miserable and now hysterical sobbing continued and even got stronger, she decided to make a grown-up decision and take Neewo from his cradle board. And so she did. She undid the twist of vine that held him inside the beaded velvet wrapping. She carefully untied and spread

the embroidered wrapping, then took out his diaper moss and brushed him off like a root pulled from the ground. He was naked, of course, but it was a warm day and so she lifted him immediately into her arms, still weeping, and brought him to a sunny place just beyond the house, behind the trees, out near the water.

Omakayas suddenly realized that Neewo had quieted. Her ears were still ringing with the sounds of his cries. Seagulls wailed, a skinny shorebird ran up and down the sand, busily pecking. Neewo brandished his chubby fists, blithered at the water, blasted spit excitedly at the sparkling waves, and turned his melting and mischief-filled eyes upon his sister to tell her that she was the most wonderful human on earth.

She settled him beside her on a warm stretch of rock. Put a stick in his hand. He looked at the stick, tested it between his gums. He had one pitiful little tooth he was very proud of, and he tried to use it to bite the stick. The stick was too strong for Neewo. He banged it purposefully at little circles of green lichen scattered on the stone's surface. When the stick broke in two, he yelled in sheer joy and continued beating the rock with the short end of it. Omakayas was so happy that she laughed out loud.

"You'll be a drummer, a singer. I'll dance for you,"

she said. Although it was wrong of her to have set Neewo free, it was very obvious that he had always wanted to be banging a stick on a rock and feeling the warm sun on his face. They sat together for a good while longer. Omakayas tossed stones in the water, sending up splashes to surprise her little brother, and he in turn seemed to try and talk to her in serious burps and babbles about what it was like to be a baby packed into a carrier, hanging on a branch all day long, never allowed to throw rocks or stuff leaves in his mouth.

Omakayas thought she heard him tell her this was the best day of his life so far. She thought she heard him tell her that she was his very favorite sister and he liked her much, much better than Angeline. He definitely said to her that he would never forget this, and that when they were very old he would stare at her the way he was doing now, and laugh, and they'd both be toothless then.

"But I have to put you back now, or else I'll get in trouble," Omakayas said. Regretfully, she lifted him into her arms, a delicious baby weight, and carried him jouncing back to the clearing and the house. As she laid him back into his wrappings and began to lace him in, his face crumpled in betrayal and he opened his mouth. Quickly, Omakayas reached into her pocket. The remains of the treat from Old Tallow was still there. She popped the last little bit of the lump of maple sugar onto his tongue. His mouth closed. A look of blissful surprise came over his face. His body relaxed. By the time Omakayas had him laced back into the tikinagun his eyelids were drooping, and by the time her mother came home with no news of her father, but with a bit of brilliant red cloth, four brass buttons, and six thimbles for which she'd traded a load of dried fish, Omakayas was rocking Neewo as though she'd been doing so all along, and her little brother was smiling in his sleep.

⊸○⊷

The month of picking heartberries went by. Little Pinch jumped off a low branch and made a huge gash just over his eye. Blood came pouring down and he seemed both proud of himself and sorry for himself, and he selfishly hogged attention for his injury to the point where Omakayas could hardly bear it. Mama was constantly preoccupied with him. Of course, that left Neewo more and more to Omakayas's hands, and she didn't mind that. After the hours they'd spent in freedom, it always seemed to Omakayas that she and her little brother exchanged a secret knowledge in their smiles.

Grandma began to call Little Pinch by a new name,

Big Pinch, because he grabbed handfuls of food and tried
to stuff his face. He was very slow learning manners. It
was hard to teach him. He had an eager, greedy, pushing
nature. Omakayas liked him less with every day that
passed, and wished desperately that someone, Old Tallow or her Auntie Muskrat, perhaps, would ask Mama if
they could keep him. When he got on her nerves the
worst, she imagined and dreamed. Maybe someone
who'd lost a son would ask for Pinch. Or maybe their
father, Mikwam, would arrive and say he needed an
always-hungry little boy of five winters to accompany
him on his next long trip. The missionaries. They might
want to use Pinch as an example—but of what? Things
not to do? He could live underneath the church. Something, anything, just a little relief! He was so annoying to
Omakayas that she found herself occasionally wishing a
dreadful wish—that an eagle or old Grandfather Owl
might snatch him up and carry him to a high nest. She
always stopped herself when her heart grew dark, but
oh, these wishes were satisfying!

◄◦►

It was a cool dark summer night in the first days of blue-
berry picking time, and Omakayas had just fallen asleep
when something made her awaken, a dream or a sound.

She lay quiet with her eyes just a tiny bit open, staring confusedly at the soft flames that occasionally flickered up among the coals that glowed in the fire pit. Omakayas raised her head, drowsy. Grandma was wedged into a thick bearskin beside the door, snoring lightly, and Big Pinch was tumbled at her feet. Angeline was tucked neatly into her blanket on the other side of the door.

Suddenly, a shiver of happiness and excitement ran down through Omakayas so strongly she feared she might cry out and wake everyone. Her heart jumped. She nearly threw off her robes to dance. Deydey, her father, was home! There, at the entrance, just barely lighted, her father's makazins were heaped with Mama's. His were worn through, dirty, beaten up, although not missing a single bead of Mama's tight beadwork. Mama's, on either side, were spruce and neat. They were her fancy ones, trimmed at the ankle with a specially prepared ruff of white rabbit fur.

Her mother's and father's makazins always had a certain way of turning toward each other, Omakayas thought. Deydey's makazins were carefully made by Mama, and sometimes worn to shreds before he got home. Soft and open, they seemed relieved to flop inside the door and nestle into the safe embrace of Mama's pair. Her makazins protected Deydey's used-up ones, nuzzled them together, and seemed to be watching over and soothing away the many dangers of his footsteps.

Drifting back into sleep, Omakayas knew that by the time she woke her mother would be cutting out a new pair of makazins from the special moose hide she herself had tanned and smoked when the heartberries were first ripening. That thought brought her back to the memory of the bear mother. As she fell back into her dreams, she wondered.

Would she tell her father what had happened? Would she ever tell anyone? Once more, she decided that she would keep the encounter to herself. Not only would she be scolded, maybe even laughed at, for playing with the bear cubs, but she was quite certain that no one else would understand.

Omakayas curled even deeper into her blanket. Smiling in delight, she buried her face in the warm fur, and fell at last into a heavy, dreamless sleep knowing when she woke there would be Father, tall, bold, strong, and joking, to swing her high in the air. Mama would laugh even more than usual. Angeline, too, shy and excited. There would be gifts, new things, special food. Grandma would cook mightily for a feast. Mama would sew on her father's makazins. Uncles would come visiting, cousins, relatives to feast and listen to stories and tease endlessly. Baby Neewo would beg with his eyes for Deydey's songs, and Big Pinch would have to be good.

CHAPTER FOUR

Andeg

 HE WORLD CHANGED when Father was home. Everyone had to be more careful and orderly. When Mama and Grandma were in charge, there was a way to do things, of course, and yet there was room to make mistakes. Mistakes were funny, and could be fixed. With Omakayas's father, Mikwam, or Ice, everything had to be done exactly right. He was a commanding person, over six feet tall and with a shrewdness in his expression that impressed other men. Often, he dressed himself quite handsomely—full turban, beaded velvet vest, calico shirt of fine red cloth, a bandolier bag, earrings. He always wore a least one fancy earring, and it glittered and spun at his jaw when he abruptly halted or changed direction in his walking.

Mikwam was very funny, and the camp was always full of laughter. But it was an uneasy laughter. At any moment, Deydey's mood could change to barbed annoyance. Much of the laughter had to do with her father's sly wit and sharp tongue. There was no one he could not imitate, no one who escaped the sharp humor of his gaze, no one about whom he could not make a joke. He even teased Old Tallow, but he loved giving her little gifts, too, and in the evenings he told stories until way after the owls began to call. With Deydey home, things were more exciting, things were more difficult, things were less predictable but somehow more secure.

First thing Deydey noticed was the corn, how tall it had grown, how the rain had plumped up the ears, what a good crop they had this year. Mama and Grandma were pleased and contented with the crop, but Deydey was jealous of the amount of new corn he saw the crows devouring. Early on the morning of the second day he was home, he cut poles and used basswood twine to rope together two platforms, one on either side of the corn-field. When he had tied the legs securely, and when he had positioned them just so, he called Angeline and Omakayas.

Andeg

"I want you to climb up and stay here and drive away the birds!" He gave Omakayas two smooth sticks to clack together to frighten the flocks, and Angeline his tattered old shirt to flap in the air.

He didn't need it anymore, for Mama had made him a new suit of clothes—a calico shirt, skin leggings, a set of blue broadcloth britches trimmed with red wool. Onto the shirt, she had sewn four carefully hoarded brass buttons, gleaming, each marked with the French flower that the voyageurs called fleur-de-lis.

Now, on a sunny day, with a sweet haze in the air and the promise of rain low and far at the edge of the horizon, Omakayas and Angeline started for the cornfield.

They argued back and forth about everything and nothing. Stubborn and bored with each other, they fell silent. The garden place lay at the end of a short path through the woods, and on the way they walked without a sound, each lost in her thoughts. Perhaps because they had fallen into that angry silence, they walked quietly enough to come upon One Horn, the magnificent buck deer who had lost half of his antler rack defending his island territory. He seemed to have damaged his head in some way so that only one of his antlers grew back properly. It was a beautiful antler, proud and pointed, but the other one was only a stump.

Unafraid of the girls, One Horn stepped out onto the path and stood alert in the early light, basking a little, warming his coat. Omakayas and Angeline stood still, held by his beauty and the strength of his gaze. His graceful, leaf-shaped ears tilted forward as though he could hear their hearts beating. His brown eyes were commanding and kind. He took a step toward them and stopped, another step, stopped, and then suddenly, as though yanked into the air by a giant invisible rope, he leaped. He disappeared.

"He must have heard something we didn't," Angeline said, and sure enough, Deydey was behind them. Right behind them with no warning.

"What's wrong with you girls?" he said, his voice sharp. "The crows are feasting while you stand here and jabber!"

He walked past them, his stride long. They hurried to the field, climbed onto their platforms, and shooed away what few birds had settled in the corn.

At first, it was fun to wave and shout across the field from their perches.

"Boozhooo," called Omakayas.

"Boozhooo," called Angeline.

"Ninoonde wesin," Omakayas yelled.

"I'm hungry, too," was the answer.

"What did you bring to eat?"

Angeline had brought nothing.

"We could roast some cooorrrrn," suggested Omakayas from across the field.

"We could roast some crowwwwwsss," cried Angeline.

"How will we catch them?" shouted Omakayas.

"I'll get Nokomis's fishing net," Angeline answered. "We'll throw it over them when they land!"

So far, not a single bird had eaten so much as a kernel of corn, because the two girls were making so much noise. But as soon as Angeline left her stand to fetch the net from Grandma, a whirling cloud descended. The smart crows and redwing blackbirds knew when their chances of getting a bite of corn had improved! The crows spread over the corn with cries of greed. Ravens, bigger and smarter, waited on the outskirts of the field to see whether it was safe to join the feast. Determined, Omakayas yelled louder and clacked her sticks. She had helped harvest each seed saved in Mama's seed bag. She had watered those seeds with water hauled from the lake, makuk after makuk of water, until they sprouted and grew. Then she had loosened the earth and weeded with Mama's big moose antler hoe and her own smaller hoe carved from a crooked tree branch. She had guided these corn plants and worked hard and she was not, now, going to give up the winter's dried corn soup to a flock of birds, no matter how hungry they were.

Again, the birds fell on the corn with starving cries. Again, Omakayas ran down screaming to drive them off. Deydey was right. The birds eyes glittered greedily as they tore into each plump ear of corn and pecked at the juicy young kernels. Their cries were ferocious. Until her sister returned, Omakayas ran from one end of the field to the other, shouting, flapping her dad's old shirt or clacking the sticks. After a time, she was too tired to run fast and her shout came out a croak as hoarse as the crows'.

Angeline returned with the net, finally, and they tried to cast it over the birds. The net worked much better at catching fish. However wide and gracefully they tried to toss it, the net always flew clumsily. The birds saw it coming, darted off, and even seemed to laugh with taunting cries as they landed, eating noisily, in another part of the field.

"We've got to trick them," Angeline said.

"Trick them how?" Omakayas panted.

"I've got an idea," said Angeline.

They draped one of Grandma's nets carefully over the cornstalks to make a ceiling. Angeline stood behind the cornstalk room with the other net held wide, and Omakayas ran to the other side of the field. When the birds landed before her, she slowly, unhurriedly, with no shouting and no sudden movements, walked toward her sister. The birds hopped before her, or flew a short distance. They were not frightened enough to wheel high in the air. They continued toward the net, and then slipped under the nets to forage, hopped further beneath, toward Angeline, until they finally ran into the wall of twines and flapped high into the ceiling of the net. In alarm, they panicked, tried to fly through the links Nokomis had woven, and caught a foot, a wing, a tiny head. Even though she had hated them just an hour before, Omakayas now felt badly about betraying them, and as she drove the birds into the net she begged them to forgive her, saying the words she had heard her grand-mother use, "Forgive us, forgive us, we have need, we have need."

She turned away as Angeline caught each strug-gling, flapping bird and broke its neck with one quick, strong twist. They harvested birds for the next hour, and the next hour, until the sun sank low and the remaining birds withdrew to their perches for the night. Then, as Omakayas was gathering in and folding Nokomis's net, she noticed one bird was left, struggling hard to free itself. It was a young crow from a late nest. Though it hopped up and down with great energy, it couldn't quite fly. They already had a pile of birds large enough to fill the biggest parching tray, which Angeline had fetched from the camp.

Omakayas decided to set this last bird free and she gently undid the basswood fiber twine from a sharp black-clawed foot, its neck, a ragged baby feathered wing. Holding the bird in her hands, she set it on the ground and waited for it to fly off. It sat still. When she tried to shoo it into the air, it only hopped a few steps, dragged a hurt wing. Omakayas looked around for a heavy stick to club it, to put it out of its pain, and then something stopped her. She looked down at the bird. It gazed up at her with such a calm, trusting curiosity that it almost seemed to speak aloud. Its round eyes were a deep milky blue, and it cocked its head sideways, back and forth, to get a good look at Omakayas. She looked around to see if Angeline was watching. She wasn't. With a swift movement, Omakayas reached down and scooped the bird into the small carrying sack at her waist. It nestled in so silently that she soon forgot all about it.

Omakayas and Angeline spent what seemed like an endless time plucking the birds, cleaning them, scorching the pinfeathers, those just growing in, too tiny to pull off. When the birds were ready to roast, Mama packed them close together along with wild onion bulbs and then pressed rich, streambed muck carefully around them. She set them in a pit in the middle of the fire and heaped live coals around the balled mound of mud. As the birds cooked, bits of steam broke through tiny cracks in the mud and scented the air with a delicious fragrance. A few ears of ripe new corn, blueberries, and a strong tea of wintergreen made the rest of the feast. When the birds were done, Mama used a stick to roll the ball of birds from the fire, and then she cracked open the baked mud. Sitting down together around the fire, they ate roasted ears of corn, sweet blueberries, and picked the delicate meat off the tiny bird bones. Each bird was no more than a few mouthfuls, hot, tasty, spiced with the oniony brown flavor. There was more than enough to fill each person, and they were all satisfied.

"These are my daughters," said Deydey, proudly. "Not only did they save the corn today, but they caught and plucked our dinner! They are hunters!"

He took his pipe from its bag to smoke it in their honor, and each girl felt a warm, proud sensation. They leaned back a little, looking into the fire, and Nokomis also took out her woman's pipe. She filled the bowl with kinnikinnick, tamped her pipe carefully, and lit it with a glowing stick.

Omakayas wanted to ask her for a story, but she knew that her Nokomis always refused, no matter how hard they begged, until the last frog was safely sleeping in the ground. Deydey, with his half-white blood, could often be persuaded because the stories he told were different from Nokomis's. Hers were adisokaan stories, meant only for winter. Deydey usually talked about his travels, the places he'd seen and the people, the close calls and momentous encounters with animals, weather, other Anishinabeg, and best of all, ghosts.

After he'd smoked his pipe, at Angeline's request Deydey spoke.

DEYDEY'S GHOST STORY

We were coming out of the rapids about two days from Boweting, in a part of the river I knew all too well, when I tasted a storm. The last thing I wanted right about then was a storm! I wanted to get my men and our canoe past that spit of land—it's shaped like a little hook and juts out into the river. The name of that place is Where the Sisters Eat. I wanted to get past it because we were hoping to catch up with a certain trader and sell to him. Besides, as I'd heard it, nobody liked to camp there at Where the Sisters Eat. Strange things happened at that place.

Still, when the sky opened and rain poured down I decided that my fears were foolish. As much as my men wanted to go on, I decided we had no choice. They grumbled, but we pulled into shore, dragged our canoes up to the drier ground under the pine trees. By then, the rain was driving down, hard. The wind was shaking the trees. There was no question of making a fire. We just had to wait it out in the cold, in the dark. So I heaped pine needles and soft branches in a bed, rolled myself underneath the canoe in my blanket. So far, everything was fine, I thought. Maybe the stories I had heard about the place were lies, things that never happened. I turned over to try and get a little sleep.

I had barely dozed off when a sudden shaft of lightning hit near, struck a tree that crashed down in the woods. All I could do was hope I had chosen a lucky spot where lightning wouldn't strike, where no tree would topple down. I should have taken my tobacco out right then and offered it up to the good spirits. I should have remembered my mother's ways. But I did not, and here is what happened after I fell asleep again, the next time I woke.

I came awake with a jolt, uneasy. Too quiet, that's the first thought I had, too quiet. No wind, no rain. No moonlight either. The clouds hung thick and heavy as a priest's black wool robe. I waved my hand in front of my face, couldn't see even the barest outline. That's how dark it was. That's when I heard them.

I heard the women arguing over bones.

There were, of course, no living women within hundreds of miles, but I was groggy and didn't think of that. All I could think of was how loud these women were talking!

"Hey, you ladies, be quiet! Someone is trying to sleep here," I called. For a little while, they lowered their voices, and then their argument broke out again and they started to shout. They had settled down to quarrel near my canoe and I was now steaming mad.

"Bekayaan!" I yelled at them, loud and harsh, to be quiet. Again, they lowered their voices, but just as soon as I got comfortable again and started to doze they broke into a loud chatter once more.

It wasn't that they sounded ugly. Their voices were high and sweet, though they were having a dis-agreement. It was just that they were so loud, and right over my head. Sitting on the canoe! I heard their weight creak on the spruce ribs.

"You be careful out there." I was getting even angrier. They took no notice of me. Just continued their excited disagreement. Here's what they said.

"You give me the first meat, Sister, you take the first bone."

"Give me the second meat, you take the first bone."

"I'll have the foot."

"I'll have the head."

"No, you won't! I'll have the head and the leg, too, Sister!"

"How shall we divide the others?"

"Let's gamble for them."

"Let's!"

"It's a good thing we raised that storm," said one of the sisters, laughing. "How else would we catch our food so easily?"

"My stomach hurts," was the answer. "It's been a long time since we caught this many!"

And then, all of a sudden, I understood. I was the first meat, the second bone! We men were the food! The ghostly sisters had come to hold their feast—us. My sweat turned cold. I remembered all too well how bothersome bad spirits were, even dangerous.

These ones had perhaps starved to death, and so were eternally hungry. They themselves had revealed how they struck up storms to force travelers to seek shelter. No wonder my men hadn't wanted to camp out on the spit of land called Where the Sisters Eat.

◄◦►

Deydey fell silent, then, and stared into the fire at the center of the wakaigun. Nobody said a word. Even Baby Neewo seemed to listen, horrified, as Deydey thought about his next move, how he would save himself from the cannibal ghosts. Deydey finally went on.

◄◦►

Here's what I did. Luckily, I thought of my father's advice. Never let fear take your mind away, he said. Always think. So instead of giving in to fear, I put fear aside and thought. And into my mind, once I let myself hear it, a plan came. Immediately, I put it into action.

Bam! Bam! I began to knock on the inside of my canoe. I huffed like a bear and shouted in a growly voice, "Wasn't he delicious, this man? Best one I ever ate!"

"Did you hear that?" said the sister above me. "A bear has eaten some of our precious food."

"How dare that bear steal from us!"

They were both furious, and to make them more furious yet I stuck the butt of my rifle out and whacked one of their feet, hard!

"Aaaaow! Aaaaow!" she cried. "Why did you hurt me, my older sister?"

"I didn't," said the older.

"Did, too," shrieked the younger. "You and that bear, always lying and greedy!"

"Me and the bear, nothing! Take that!"

"AAAAOOOWWW!"

◄○►

Deydey gave a horrifying shriek that made the skin on Omakayas's neck crawl, heart jolt, scalp tighten with fear. She snuggled deeper into the blankets and robes next to Grandma, who held her tight.

"AAAAAOOOOWWWHHHHH!"

Again, Deydey gave his version of the ghostly shriek. Big Pinch covered his head and crashed into Mama's lap. Deydey let a silence fall and then told the ending in a hushed, spooky tone.

◄○►

The two sisters began to hit at each other, first

with their fists, then with sticks, then with rocks pulled from the ground. While they were occupied with trying to kill each other, I loaded my canoe quick as could be. I could hear the others doing the same. No doubt, listening to the sisters plan to eat us, the men had been shaking in their blankets. Just as we were pushing off, one of the sisters noticed us leaving and with a scream she bounded toward us. I was the last one out, steering from behind. I shouted to my men, "Paddle, men, paddle hard!" Still, the evil sister managed to grab my shirt and rip it almost into shreds. Just see!

◄◦►

Deydey solemnly produced the pieces of shirt that his daughters had used to frighten off the birds that day. Big Pinch gasped and the girls were silent. "Yes," said Deydey, "it was lucky I got out of there alive. And do you know, after I hit the ghost with my gun barrel, the gun split on me, refused to let me fix it! Fortunately, we did catch up with that trader who always made such a good price to us. And luckily, too . . . ."—Deydey drew out the last word teasingly, which made the girls ears perk with interest—"luckily, I was able to trade for a few small things." Deydey drew a little cloth-wrapped package from inside his shirt.

He opened the package with such care that Omakayas thought he might have brought back a live thing,
perhaps a small squirrel, or maybe—she momentarily
recalled the tiny bird in her carrying sack, was it even
still in the corner? Probably it was quite dead by now.
Omakayas felt a pang. She focused again on Deydey's
gift. He loved giving gifts, drawing out the suspense, and
he always chose wonderful things. This time, he drew
from his small sack a long, thick band of indigo ribbon
for Angeline. For Mama, a precious dress length of calico
cloth, deep red with blue and pink flower sprigs all over
it. For Grandma, tobacco, a big twist of it, golden brown.
Big Pinch received a small knife and Baby Neewo one
tiny piece of velvet to lay against his soft cheek. As for
Omakayas, something special was in store, said Deydey.
Something he had made himself. She caught her breath.

"Na," he said, "here. This is for you!"

He handed her the sawed-off length of his gun
barrel, the one that ruined itself after he struck the
ghost sister's feet. The end of the gun barrel was pinched
together with tongs and given a rough, sharp edge. It
was clearly, Omakayas gulped to see it, a hide scraper.

"When Mama showed me what a good job you'd
done on that moose hide for my makazins," said Deydey,
"I decided you should have my old gun barrel for your

own first scraping tool. The skins you prepared for my makazins are very fine. From now on, I want you to prepare skins often for Mama and for me. Take this," he said.

Omakayas was confused. Pride fought with dismay inside of her, and she took the gun-barrel hide flesher from her father with a conflicted heart. Preparing hides—her most hated work! And now, just because she had done a good job one time, she was picked out, special, for the rest of her life. She would be condemned to soften, tan, work with stinking hides. "No!" she wanted to say, "I won't take it. I want a ribbon like Angeline's, only red maybe, or yellow! Cloth, please, a bit of sweetness. A licorice stub. Anything. Anything else at all!"

But she took Deydey's gift with a tender thanks, knowing how much he delighted in choosing the presents, and how rarely he praised.

Almost resentfully, she looked over at Deydey's new makazins. Surrounded and held by Mama's makazins, they looked fresh, neat, new. Omakayas had to admit—the hide she had tanned was beautiful.

Suddenly, her heart thumped. Her throat shut. Owah! Deydey's makazin. Oh, she was sure she saw it move. It had moved. She was sure of it. Again!

"Neshkey!" Her voice trembled. She pointed. The others looked.

This time, the makazin took a big hop forward and everyone, even Deydey, cried out in surprise. They were all frozen in shock. The makazin sat quiet, still. Nokomis leaned over, poked at it with a stick. The makazin twitched. Then squawked. Omakayas jumped up, for she remembered instantly that she'd left her carrying sack right next to the door with the makazins. Sure enough, her bird popped its head out, bright, and in the sound of everyone's laughter it blinked with interest, cheerful, greedy, hungry, unafraid.

Dagwaging

(FALL)

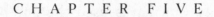

CHAPTER FIVE

Fishtail's Pipe

OW IN THE MORNINGS there was a sharp freshness in the air. Omakayas loved this time of the year and jumped from her blankets eagerly, rolled her sleeping mat and fur blanket, and put them away quickly so that she could help rekindle the outdoor cooking fire. Her crow hopped after her. Though it could fly short distances, its wing hadn't yet healed. Andeg, the Anishinabe or Ojibwa word for crow, was its name. Nokomis was fond of Andeg. The bird often rode on her shoulder and kept her company as she packed dry fish, repaired nets, wove new mats, and, alongside Omakayas, tanned hides they needed now for winter clothing—jackets, makazins, mittens, hoods. Omakayas used the gun-barrel flesher, Deydey's gift. She didn't like the work any better than she ever had, but Andeg's lively company helped. Andeg even frightened off an owl, and once, perched on the head guard of baby Neewo's cradle board, *craackacraccked* loudly and repeatedly until Mama came running to find a curious raccoon trying to steal from the bundles of dried fish and venison she was preparing to cache. Andeg quickly became everybody's favorite. But the crow slept only near Omakayas. He fell asleep just at dusk, perching low on a branch she had tied into the side of the ribs of the birchbark house.

—◄○►—

Deydey spent a few warm fall days making repairs on his canoe, and then it was time for him to leave again. He would make one more big trip before the cold rains, and then the harsh snow, slashed down. Once he stopped gathering and selling the furs of other Anishinabeg, he would go out on his own trapline. For the rest of the late fall and winter he would be home and gone, home and gone, and each time he returned, Omakayas thought with a sinking stomach, he would be hauling back skins for her to work on.

One afternoon, his friends and partners came to

visit and make their plans. Albert LaPautre and Fishtail came walking through the woods. When Angeline and Omakayas saw the men coming, they decided to hide and quickly dived into a heavy stand of bush. Peeking between weedy stalks, they had a good view. Albert was round as a kettle and his big teeth stuck out pleasantly when he grinned. He fancied himself quite a medicine man and wore at his throat a circle of bear claws. Next to him walked the tall and handsome Fishtail. He had strikingly long, thick, oiled black hair, and a hawk-thin face with a proud curl to his lips. He carried his pipe in the cradle of his left arm, close to his heart.

It was a fancy pipe, made of a piece of sumac wood marked with a sweet grain. Bands along the stem were carefully beaded in black and yellow. Fishtail took extremely good care of his pipe, cleaned it often, prayed with it every sunrise. To him, it was a living thing. The bowl was red pipestone in the shape of an otter's head, his clan. Dark blue pony beads hung down a swatch of fringe, and Fishtail touched them carefully and lovingly as he stepped quietly along.

Mikwam came out along the path to meet his friends, and the men talked and joked before they made themselves comfortable, sitting on blankets on the ground. Omakayas saw her father open up his leather pouch of sweet kinnikinnick and asema, or tobacco. Fishtail lit the pipe, and the fragrance of burning red-willow tobacco hung peacefully in the air. Each man, as he drew in the smoke, wore a look of concentrated and peaceful attention. The pipe passed around the circle twice before any of the men said a word.

What they said made Omakayas and Angeline creep closer, listen more carefully. Hidden in the grass and underbrush, they breathed quietly and opened their ears to catch the lower tones of the men's voices.

"Chimookoman," said Fishtail, in a growling tone of indignation. The word meant "big knife," and it was

used to describe the non-Indian, or white people, who were traveling in larger numbers than ever to Ojibwa land and setting down their cabins, forts, barns, gardens, pastures, fences, fur-trading posts, churches, and mission schools. LaPointe was becoming more chimookoman every day, and there was talk of sending the Anishinabeg to the west.

"They say we must leave the island," Fishtail went on.

No one commented. Curled against itching nettle leaves, Omakayas eased her hand to her leg to scratch. She scratched silently and kept listening.

"That's right," her father said at last, contempt in his voice, "that's what they are saying. The useless ones."

Albert LaPautre drew on the pipe and frowned, tamping and adjusting the tobacco burning in the bowl. He drew deep and puffed hard. He was part French, like Deydey, but browner than Fishtail. His eyes were greenish-brown. His round, cheerful face beamed. He sighed, and with a faraway look said that he had a vision. Fishtail and Deydey looked blankly and patiently at him when he said this, for LaPautre was known for recounting visions and dreams that had very little meaning, though they seemed to affect him hugely. Now he looked down sternly, gathering his thoughts. Suddenly, he blurted out, "I dreamed I had lice!"

In the brush, Angeline and Omakayas clapped hands over their mouths to stifle their glee. Deydey and Fishtail managed to keep straight faces, but Omakayas was sure she saw the corner of Deydey's mouth twitch.

Albert LaPautre sighed. "The meaning is unclear," he muttered.

"Let us find the meaning," said Deydey. His voice was serious, but the girls both knew that he was having fun with LaPautre. "Was anything else happening in your dream?"

LaPautre frowned, as though overcome with the weight of his vision. "Yes," he said, "we were planning a dance gathering!"

"Ah!" said Father, "the meaning now becomes clear! This was a deep dream, indeed!"

"What?" LaPautre was breathless.

"From now on when you dance," Father said, without allowing the trace of a smile, "you will dance hard enough to shed your lice."

"Yes?" LaPautre's voice was suspicious, but neither Deydey nor Fishtail let on by any sign that Father's interpretation was a joke.

"Perhaps," said LaPautre, "I should tell you my own thoughts." And then, to Angeline and Omakayas's surprise and dismay, he told the other men that he was thinking of taking his family, all ten of his children, his uncles and grandmas and grandpas, to a western post where, he had heard, government payments were made.

Omakayas nudged Angeline. Those children were

their friends. To think that they might have to leave! Omakayas nearly cried out, but Angeline poked her to be quiet.

All of the Ojibwa would be safe on their own land farther west, Albert was saying. No one would bother them. Yes, there were hazards on the way—Dakota war parties, hunger, the threat of winter's dire weather. He'd rather not go. Still, said jolly Albert, he had moved before when the waves of white people lapped his feet.

"West, always west," said Deydey, agreeing slowly. "We hear the chimookoman ax ring in the woods, chopping a tree. We should be gone before the tree falls."

"We have to stop somewhere, someday." Fishtail drew thoughtfully on the pipe and the fragrant smoke clouded his face. "West is where the spirits of the dead walk. If the whites keep chasing us west, we'll end up in the land of the spirits."

"I have dreamed that's where they want us to go, anyway," said Albert. "That will please them."

"They are like greedy children. Nothing will ever please them for long," said Deydey. Although his grandfather had been French, he was raised and considered himself Ojibwa and kept the rules of his mother's dodem or clan, the catfish clan. The Awausesee. Only in some chimookoman things, his cabin for instance, and his ability to play and win the white man's game of chess with the trader, did he take secret pride.

"Not until they have it all," said Fishtail. "All of our lands. Our wild-rice beds, hunting grounds, fishing streams, gardens. Not even when we are gone and they have the bones of our loved ones will they be pleased. I have thought about this."

Fishtail put up his hand and held it there, looked keenly at his friends. "Before they were born, before they came into this world, the chimookoman must have starved as ghosts. They are infinitely hungry."

The men smoked with increased intensity, looking deep into the fire as the breeze came up and dusk lowered. Deydey was thoughtful, his eyes deep and clouded.

Even LaPautre looked serious, the dimples set hard in his cheeks. Watching in the bushes, Omakayas and Angeline waited for them to resume their talking, but that day, mulling over Fishtail's difficult words perhaps, the men kept their silence.

CHAPTER SIX

Pinch

IG PINCH GOT IN trouble and Omakayas was glad. Here's how it happened.

One day, Mama found a bush of late-bearing chokecherries. They were plump, and so ripe that they had turned a deep blackish-purple color. She picked until her fingers turned red-black at the tips. When she returned, bearing her load of berries, Mama's eye lit on Big Pinch.

"I have a job for you," she said. His eyes got beady and his lip turned out. He pouted at her, but she paid his lowered looks no mind.

"I'm spreading these berries on the bark sheaves so they will dry," she went on, and then she proceeded to spread out the berries on clean birchbark, in the warmest patch of sun she could find. "You watch them carefully now, Big Pinch. Keep the birds away. Listen, my son." Mama narrowed her eyes at Pinch so that he would know he was trusted with an important task. "This is our winter seasoning and food. You'll be glad of them when we are hungry in little spirit moon."

She gave Big Pinch a long, ferny branch to wave and made him sit next to the berries. Then she turned her back on him and went out to the lake with Grandma to check their fish nets. She took Neewo along with her, put him carefully in his tikinagun, petted and kissed him. Angeline and Omakayas were sent to town. They were to sweep out and prepare the family cabin for the winter move. Big Pinch was left alone.

◄o►

It was hard being Big Pinch, harder than his sisters would ever know. They didn't understand how good it felt to fill a stomach that so rarely got full. They didn't realize how good it felt to shove handfuls of berries into his greedy mouth. Pinch looked at the berries. Bored, he shooed away a few small chickadees. Andeg sat with him, on a low branch. But Andeg knew better than to eat the berries. If only, thought Pinch sadly, those berries didn't look *so delicious*! Mama had found a patch of chokecherries that were much more luscious than most. These were the biggest, fattest berries Pinch had ever seen! It didn't seem as though it would hurt to eat a few. Pinch sneaked one, then a few more, then a handful. Andeg cawed three times, and seemed to disapprove. Pinch made a face at the bird. The berries tasted as good as they looked, better. Richer, blacker, without that mouth-puckering chokecherry taste. He might just have another handful.

Well, he thought not long after he finished that bunch, a handful more would not hurt. And then, just to balance the look of the berries, he took more from one side. The other. He spread the berries out and then the bark looked full again. Pinch waited. The sun blossomed

slowly, so slowly, and it took such a long time to dry the berries. Pinch tried to amuse himself, but with nobody there to bother, he was at a loss. Andeg didn't want to play and flew out of reach. There was nobody to annoy except himself!

Another handful. Another and another. Pinch rearranged the berries once again. Now there seemed to be plenty of berries on the bark—they were well spaced, it was true, but the bark sheaves looked full. He kept nibbling, spacing, arranging, and rearranging until sleep overcame him and he curled up tight and nodded away.

◄o►

"Pinnnnnch!" It was Mama's threatening voice. She was standing tall over the berries and she wasn't the least bit fooled by Pinch's berry arrangement. "What happened? Where are the berries I picked, you sleepy boy!"

Pinch woke, jumped up rubbing his eyes, blinking. It was true! There were very few berries on the bark sheaves. Had he eaten so many? How could he? Big Pinch was horrified, embarrassed at himself.

"Pinnnchhhh!" Mama was using her very angry voice now, and Pinch felt so terrible that his brain raced and he seized suddenly upon a blaming lie.

"Andeg ate them. Bad Andeg!"

Pinch pointed up and sure enough, Andeg, sitting out of reach on a high branch, certainly looked guilty as he glared down and preened his new growth of feathers. Mama, furious that her work was all for nothing, shook her fist in the air and called out to Andeg.

"Come on down and eat the rest of them!"

Andeg, not understanding, hopped down to nearly within her reach and cocked his head in a friendly way as though to inquire, "Are you sure?"

"AAAAYyaaaah!"

Mama took Andeg's friendliness as a sign that he really had eaten up the berries. Mama grabbed a stick, shook it hard. Andeg croaked in alarm. With a shout, she threw back her arm, took sudden aim at the bird, and hurled the stick at Andeg.

"CaaaaaH!" Andeg was hit. Although not seriously hurt, he jumped fearfully from branch to branch and fluttered out of reach, then farther, farther away, until he was lost from view.

"See what you made me do?" Mama called, but immediately she sat down, sorry, knowing that the fault lay strictly with herself. "I must get the better of myself. I must. I must." She shook her head. "How could I?" Now her daughter's pet was frightened, and even if he had eaten all of the berries she worked so hard to pick, Mama loved the crow and never meant to scare him. How betrayed by humans the bird must feel, she thought guiltily. And here she had trained him to eat from her hand! Now he was frightened off.

"Come back," she called hopefully into the woods. "Ombay!"

But the bird, still crying out in confusion, only fled deeper into the woods. Mama sat down sadly, ashamed of herself. That was how Omakayas found her mother when she returned from her town errand. Mama told what had happened, how Andeg had eaten the berries Pinch was watching, and how she had gotten angry, frightened Andeg off, how she was now sorry to have done so and would help Omakayas find the bird.

"Surely, he will come to you," said Mama.

Just as she was explaining why it was she had lost her temper and how hard she had worked to find those berries, Big Pinch groaned.

"What's wrong?" Mama asked.

"Oooooh." Big Pinch lay down holding his stomach. "It hurts. Oooooh. It hurts."

"Saaa!"

Mama bent over her boy, inspecting him. "A stomachache, eh?" She was immediately suspicious.

Gently but firmly, she took his hands in hers, uncurled them, saw the telltale juice marks of bruised choke-cherries that darkened his fingertips, then the pitiful, berry-stained smile that sealed his guilt!

"Pinch," she said, and this time her voice was worse than angry. It was disappointed. "You lied. The ghost foot carries off liars in the night! As for your stomachache, there is no medicine but enduring the consequences of your greed. You'll have to suffer, Pinch. Maybe this will teach you!"

With that, she and Omakayas left him to Angeline and went off into the woods seeking Andeg.

◄o►

Not far into the woods, they heard Andeg's distinctive croak. "Craawk! Craaawkacraak!"

"There!" said Mama, pointing. "You go to him, Omakayas. He doesn't trust me, and I don't blame him." She gave Omakayas a crust of bannock bread, a treat, and sent her ahead, although she stayed within sight should Omakayas need her. And something happened, sure enough, that made Mama glad she stayed close, though she couldn't have explained it if she tried.

Far ahead, she heard branches cracking, and a sound she knew well, a low chuffing. Bears. High in the oak trees, stuffing themselves with acorns, the tubby young bears moved along the thinnest branches. More crashing. Now a squeal. One of the bears ventured out too far, curious, and tumbled right out of the tree. He picked himself up, and stood on his hind legs. His acorn-chubby belly stuck out like LaPautre's. Then Mama saw both little bears loping and bounding through the woods toward Omakayas.

"Daughter!" she shouted. Bears are shy, and these wouldn't seek Omakayas out to attack, surely. On the other hand, they could be dangerous, especially if wounded or angered. Mama ran toward Omakayas, but then stopped, afraid to disturb what took place. The two young bears bounded curiously toward her daughter. She saw Omakayas turn sharply to the bears, and then, after a moment of surprise, Omakayas greeted the animals. She stood quietly before them, and she was smiling! Mama was further surprised and frightened when without a sound of warning a huge sow bear fattened for winter rambled out of the brush and passed Omakayas without acknowledging her, a human, as the least bit strange or out of place. And the younger bears, was she talking to them? Mama couldn't see. She crept nearer and listened to what her daughter said.

"Ahneen, neshemay," she said to the nearest one. "You've gotten fat!" She smiled at their bumbling, chubby bodies. They were huge! Over the summer, they had grown until they outweighed her by a great deal, though they still were bashful and hung back, just beyond the reach of her fingertips, as she spoke to them.

"So, you're getting ready to sleep," she said, offering the bannock pieces. "Here, my brothers, sleep well!"

The bears stood before her, testing the air, the unfamiliar smell of the bannock, and then each one bent to the bit of bread she held, flicked it up with a muscular tongue, and loped off into the woods behind their mother, who was clearly just a little tired of them following her along, and grumpy because she wanted to sleep.

◄○►

Andeg returned that evening to sit just outside the circle of the outdoor cooking fire. He hopped a little closer when Omakayas tempted him with a bit of stew meat. He never did trust Mama again, though, never did perch near and watch her at work, tipping his head side to side as though he were learning her actions. He still warned her of all approaching animals or strangers, but he was wary of her ever after she lost her temper, and kept his distance, which made her sad. Andeg did, however, perform a great service in the winter cabin.

While Omakayas dragged kettle after kettle of mud to the side of the cabin and, along with Angeline, chinked the cracks that had opened during hot weather, Andeg hunted. His vigilance and hatred for mice helped the whole family in their efforts to ready the cabin for winter. He chased mice, tried to pounce on them, swept them away with his wings, even caught a few and pecked them sharply, as though to warn them. And they never did come back. They sought other cabins and wigwams, where there was not a frightful crow to bother them.

◄○►

Now it was time to harvest the wild rice that grew across from the island in the great sloughs of Kakagon, where Mama's brother and one of her sisters lived. It was a part of the year everyone looked forward to because there would be cousins to play with, games in the rice camps, the pleasures of talk, feasting, more talk, more visiting and feasting. Early in the morning, then, they all set out in the canoe they had worked on a year ago. It was beautifully made, light and strong, carefully water-proofed with pitch by Grandma, who kept it in good repair and in its own house by the side of the lake. They all got in—Mama in back to paddle and steer, Grandma up front taking turns with Angeline, who held Neewo in his cradleboard. They all fit into the canoe with plenty of room to spare. That space, they hoped, they would fill with the wild rice, the manomin, the good seed that would sustain them through the winter.

Omakayas envied her big sister. She wanted to hold and play with her smiling baby brother. Neewo had a second tooth and seemed even prouder of it than the first. Omakayas had saved a bit of hard bannock bread for him to chew on, and she put it in his mouth. Neewo never even bit her. Omakayas put her finger to his cheek, stroked it softly. Why, oh why, did she have to take care of Big Pinch? She sighed, and turned to him. She was in charge of Pinch, or he was in charge of her—she wasn't sure which because it was one of his mischief days when nothing she could do would satisfy him. Andeg, perched on Omakayas's shoulder, was set-tled in for the long ride, and sympathetic to Omakayas. He knew that Pinch had something to do with the bad day Mama had lost her temper.

Before they started out, Grandma gave her tobacco

to the water and asked for a safe, smooth crossing. The
sun was mild and the waves low, the wind fresh but still
warm, and things would have gone perfectly if Pinch
hadn't teased Andeg. But he did. Every time he thought
no one was looking, he tried to pull a feather out of
Andeg's tail.

"Gaygo, Pinch," said Omakayas.

"Gaygo, Pinch," said Angeline.

"Gaygo, Pinch," said Mama, when he tried again.

"Gaygo, Pinch," said Grandma, wearily.

"Gaygo, Pinch," said Omakayas again.

They must have said it more times as they traveled
the lake than there were waves or fish alongside of
them! They said it so many times they didn't hear themselves anymore. Stop it, Pinch! Gaygo, Pinch! Stop it!
Stop! Same as when they said it onshore, Pinch didn't
hear it. He just kept trying to pull a feather. Finally,
Pinch got ahold of the black tip of Andeg's pride and joy,
his tail.

"Gaygo, Pinch!"

Everyone gasped. This time it was Andeg who spoke!

Terrified at the crow's harsh croak, Pinch nearly
threw himself out of the canoe, nearly tipped them all
over in his panic to get to Mama, who yelled, of course,
"Gaygo, Pinch!" causing Andeg to flap his wings and say

again, "Gaygo, Pinch!" which made Pinch cry, an embarrassment he never quite got over. From then on he regarded Andeg with stubborn awe, treated the bird with reserved respect, and in fact behaved just a little better, for just a little while, as Nokomis told him that his rascal ways annoyed even the animals!

"Wait until you hear what Mukwah, the bear, says, or Grandfather Owl! Think of that!" Nokomis scolded.

Pinch didn't want to.

◄◦►

When they reached the river's entrance and paddled toward the rice camp, Grandma noted with disappointment the thinness of the rice stalks. Too much standing water in the spring had caused them to grow too quickly. Some of the rice heads drooped right over into the water. She frowned. The season would be a poor one, unless the water in the other rice beds had been lower. They reached the shores of the camp, and there, amid the general happiness at seeing one another, the grown-ups learned the rice was indeed sparse that year. This was not good news, but the children could not have cared less. Nothing ruined their fun! Immediately, Omakayas raced off, her crow flapping alongside her, to find her cousins and introduce them to her friend Andeg.

There under the tree, she saw Wishkob's daughters, Little Bee and Twilight, and her cousins, including Tatah, a thin and quiet boy just a little younger than Omakayas. He was the son of her mother's brother Akewaynzee. As soon as Omakayas saw Tatah, an itchy, joking mood always came upon her and she looked around to see what tricks she could play on her quiet cousin. His older brothers were rough and ran wild, and he had a sister known as a strong, swift runner. Her name was Two Strike Girl, and she was better than most boys at hunting and fighting. She had to be forced to do the things girls normally did, and her mother and grandma had finally given up on her.

"I'm dancing the rice this year!" Two Strike Girl told Omakayas right off. That was most often the boys' job, but she had persuaded the rice chief she could do it.

◄◦►

Early the next morning, the rice boss blessed the harvest and Mama set out with Auntie Muskrat, who poled in back while Mama used her rice sticks to bend the stalks toward her and knock the rice grains off into the bottom of the boat. That year, although the harvest was not the best, there was rice for everyone and, as always, work that could not be avoided. Omakayas grumbled when Grandma asked her to go pick reeds.

"Take Two Strike Girl with you," she ordered. "Pick enough for two mats."

So Omakayas and her cousin went to the side of the slough where the flattest reeds grew, and used their knives to slice them off below the waterline, bunch after

bunch, until they had great bundles that they carried back to camp on their shoulders.

"Here," said Two Strike Girl, dumping hers off. She gathered herself to spring away, but Grandma caught her.

"Stay," ordered Grandma, "help your cousin weave."

Two Strike Girl looked alarmed, and then horrified at the idea of doing girl's work. Still, because she was ordered to do it by Grandma, she sat down beside Omakayas and began to weave the reeds into strong, simple mats that they would use to smoke the rice. Even now, the great fire Mama had prepared was burning down to its embers, and as the girls' fingers moved unwillingly, Pinch was just as unwillingly gathering up rotten old pieces of maple wood to use in smoking the rice.

When he had gathered several sagging piles of the crumbly maple wood, and when the mats were finished, Omakayas's regular and straight in its weave, and Two Strike Girl's crooked and gaping, Mama took the mats and set them over the smoking maple fire. Then, on top of the mats, she poured the rice, which began, after the mat was properly heated, to give off a most delicate, nutty aroma. Using a rake made from a stick of red willow pulled up by the roots, the two girls took turns turning the rice over and over, smoking and toasting the grains. As the rice cooked, it gathered the taste of the maple.

"I can't take this anymore!" cried Two Strike Girl, throwing down the stick. "If I have to work, at least I'm going to have some fun at it!"

Running over to a bark-lined pit in the ground, she jumped in and began treading rice with a frantic pace that made everyone around her laugh. It was the sight of the impatient Two Strike Girl dancing the rice that Omakayas would remember long after, in the deep winter of the year. Her face was flushed and thrilled with effort. She was tireless. All day, and the next, Two Strike's legs moved up and down, her feet, in clean new makazins, crushed the tough hulls. She never stopped. And all the time her eyes were shining, her white teeth set in a huge grin. Andeg danced up and down with her on a limb above.

"Come help me," she called to Omakayas. Jumping to help her cousin, Omakayas felt as proud and bold. The two held hands and stepped high, day after day, night after night. Although the family did not return with as much rice as they needed, Omakayas and Two Strike Girl became such good friends that, ever after, they called each other sister.

CHAPTER SEVEN

The Move

EYDEY LEFT ON HIS VOYAGE, and the rest of the family worked hard to prepare as much food as possible for the winter. For days, the girls dried and then parched the corn that they had saved from the hungry birds. Around and around they stirred the corn in an iron kettle over a low fire. Nokomis went over to Tallow's place and pounded some of the corn to meal with the hollowed log and great round stick that Tallow kept in her yard. While Nokomis worked on the corn, Tallow gutted fish and dried them on a big scaffold that she set up over a special fire she would feed day and night with cedarwood to give the fish a special flavor. The charcoal from the cedar she would keep to mix with pine pitch. Mixed together, the stuff made caulking for the seams of their canoes.

At the winter cabin, Deydey had built a rough lean-to and attached it alongside the northern wall. Inside the log lean-to, he had dug out a deep, round hole. Angeline and Mama spent one morning lining the earth of the hole with birchbark. They made a tight bark container, like a big makuk, and lined that container with bunches of dried grass. Then they took more curved pieces of birch-bark and set them in the interior. This was their food cache. Within the cache, Mama first placed several packs of dried, smoked fish and venison, all tied carefully together in two layers of bark. When those packs were set neatly down on the bottom, she told Omakayas to fetch the parched corn, which she had stored in neat skin bags. There were several makuks of wild rice from the fall's gathering, though the harvest had been so poor. Mama had used the intestines of the moose to store the pounded meat and dried berries they would have on feast days as a treat. She set those very carefully to one side, surrounded by sheaves of bark. Deep, deep in the food cache, unseen to anyone but Omakayas, Mama set eight birchbark cones of maple sugar. These, Omakayas knew, were for the hardest times in winter, when they would need sweetness to survive in spirit, as well as food to keep them strong.

When all was finished, Nokomis came to bless the cache.

In the deep light of the fading afternoon, Grandma raised her arms, the way she did at sunrise near the water. Everything grew very quiet around her. Even Pinch stopped shuffling his feet and rubbing his nose. Outside, the birds hushed. The sky bent to listen. The wind died down. Golden leaves hung balanced in the air. It was as though, Omakayas thought, all of creation was interested in Nokomis's words. Even her own heart beat quieter, and that excited, jumpy feeling in her calmed. Whenever Grandma prayed, she made the world around her feel protected, safe, eternal.

Nokomis bent over and looked very carefully at the cache to make certain that it was properly packed.

"Anishaa," she breathed quietly, standing again, holding in her palm a tiny mound of tobacco. She looked down at the tobacco, touched it lovingly, and asked the spirits for protection against the cold. She spoke to the creator. "We're very small," she said, "just human. Help us to live this winter through. Come to us, especially, during the harshest moon, the Crust On The Snow Moon, when so often meat is scarce, when the ice is too thick to catch many fish, when disease breaks us and the windigo spirit, the Hungry One, comes stalking from house to Anishinabe house. Oh, daga, wedookaow Anishinabeg. Wedookaow Anishinabeg," she asked.

Her voice was soft, but deep and troubled. Stillness swirled about the little cabin when she finished. It was as though everyone's heart were touched a little by the coming cold, as though a shadow of the windigo swept across their minds. Omakayas shivered. Angeline touched her shoulder. Mama stroked Pinch's rough, haylike stack of hair. Baby Neewo was the first to make a sound, and that sound was a sudden cry.

<o>

They spent that last night in the birchbark house, chilled in their robes and blankets. Already, Omakayas missed summer. When morning came, Mama hardly had the fire going before they all began to pack. Mama stirred the soup in the kettle, heated it through, and brought some to Nokomis in the tin bowl, with the trader's spoon. Nokomis drank it all up, stretched her arms, hopped to her feet with a young girl's agility. She rubbed her hands. She loved moving, packing, changing locations. Before the sun even popped its rays through the lowest brush, she was carefully rolling up the rush mats she had woven. From the inside walls of the house, she lifted down her careful bundles of roots, her bags of berries and dried, crumbled leaves, and long curls of inner bark of certain trees.

For the first time, Omakayas noticed all of these little bundles, how cleverly they were tied. How interesting each one smelled. Their colors, their odd, shriveled shapes. She helped Nokomis take the bundles down, put them carefully in her net to carry.

"I'll take them," she said, her arms full.

"We'll go together," said Nokomis, watching with interest as Omakayas touched a particular root, sniffed a tiny packet and sneezed, rubbed a powder with her finger.

"Are they talking to you?" Nokomis asked, curious, as they walked along the trail soon after. "Do you hear their voices?"

"No," said Omakayas, startled. "I don't hear anything!"

After a while, as they walked the trail, as the medicines grew heavy, she thought to ask:

"Nokomis, do they talk to *you*?"

She nodded. "Yes, sometimes they tell me things, but of course, I have learned how to listen."

"What do they tell you?"

"How to use them when someone is sick, where to find them, how to prepare them just the right strength. I wondered if they had picked you to talk to, my granddaughter. I've been watching how quiet you are sometimes. Your mama told me about the bear cubs in the woods."

"Oh, *they* talk to me," Omakayas said, laughing a little at the memory of their peculiar, sleepy, stubborn looks at their mother, so like Pinch when he didn't want to go to bed.

"Listen to them." Nokomis stopped in the path. Holding her bundles in her arms, she gazed at Omakayas until, understanding the gravity of Nokomis's nature, Omakayas stood still. Holding the medicines and looking curiously at her grandmother, she waited.

"Listen to them," was all Nokomis said, touching Omakayas's face. She spoke so earnestly, with such emotion in her voice, that Omakayas was always to remember that moment, the bend in the path where they stood with the medicines, her grandmother's kind face and the words she spoke.

◄○►

By the end of the day, the cabin was once again their home. Neewo slept in his winter bed, a blanket fixed on the ropes so that he could gently rock to sleep. Mama had a fire going in the fire pit, a small hearth that Deydey had made for them of the smoothest, thickest, heaviest stones. Omakayas was always glad to see that hearth once the fire was lighted, for she spent many cold winter nights huddled near, in blankets, listening to Grandma and gazing so long at the patterns in the lake rocks that she saw things—faces, animals—and had come to know them as familiar. That night in their cabin, it was at first too warm to cuddle in a blanket, so she sat on the mat on the earth floor and watched the flames throw shadows leaping across the stones.

There—a long-legged racing dog, a face of an old woman, a raccoon's face, a frog, Omakayas' namesake. She greeted them drowsily, old friends, and fell asleep against her grandma. Halfway through the night, Omakayas woke, freezing. She patted around the floor until she found her blanket, then she snuggled quickly in, for the cold had crept with iron stealthiness into the cabin. Dark air stabbed at them from all along the edges of the sleeping mats. It seized at their shoulders, their feet, even the hair on top of Omakayas's head and the tip of her nose. She buried her face in the fur of her blanket, nestled close against Nokomis's back, and as she fell asleep it seemed to her that there was something odd in the ferocity of the cold that continued to deepen as the night went on. She never quite warmed, kept shifting as cold drafts seized a foot or iced her knees. All night, she woke, slept, woke again, and it took until the darkness lightened before she felt warm enough to drop into a heavy dream.

CHAPTER EIGHT

First Snow

 HE AIR IN THE CABIN was brilliant; there was a flash to the light that told her it had snowed while she slept! The first snow!

"Aayah!" Pinch screamed, throwing off his rabbit-skin blanket to run outside.

"Don't slide on the lake yet!" Mama knew what he was up to, and raced to the door after him to stop him from running straight out onto the ice. Although the cold was sudden and the snow had fallen thick and mysterious overnight, the water of the lake was still open just past a skim of delicate ice onshore. Already the air was warming up a little, at least where the sun shone brightest. Mama was worried that Deydey would not manage to make the crossing before the freeze-up. If he didn't, if he couldn't, he would have to wait in camp until the ice was solid and he and his men could pull their toboggans of stretched furs across to sell to the traders.

Down the cleared path now, striding large, feather nodding in time with each long step, came Old Tallow. She held her long rifle loosely under one arm, and growled her Ahneen at Omakayas as she tramped into the brush. Omakayas called back, and Old Tallow's hand went up in an abrupt wave, though she didn't turn to look or certainly to smile. Her dogs followed at her heels, great and wolvish. The slinking yellow dog paused to turn and bare its broken brown teeth at Omakayas, but she crossed her eyes at him and couldn't have cared less. First snow day always lifted her out of her skin, made her feel sharp and alive.

The snow, not deep, softening, gleamed in a white cover over all that she could see. Each branch was neatly outlined, and some still bore their leaves. Omakayas and Angeline admired the intricate way that the snow trimmed the dried reeds of cattails and the brown furry heads were capped with tiny white mounds that made them look . . .

"Delicious, minopogwud!" Angeline pretended to bite.

"Take this!" Not only was Pinch annoying, but he had a good aim. Just as Omakayas turned she caught a firm-packed snowball on the side of her face. The snow stung. Pinch had packed a little stone in it! The wet snow licked her neck. Omakayas ran at him without a word and threw herself on him, buried him face first in a mound of snow directly beside the path.

"Gaygo!" Pinch howled and leaped up, mad, packed more snowballs together and set off after his laughing sisters. The more he ran on his short legs, though, the faster they galloped ahead. There was not a chance that he would catch them. He knew it, and finally stopped. He slumped down near the side of the path, muttering to himself and putting more snowballs together until he had a big pile. At the heart of each, he packed a stone. Stones he hoped would sting his sisters until they cried!

◄○►

The girls walked farther into the town, knowing Mama was busy, hoping she wouldn't miss them quite yet. It was exciting to live around other people again, and both of the girls wanted to find out if old friends had stayed to winter. They wanted to see if any new families had come to live near. Angeline was thinking of going to the Catholic mission school, and she wanted to sneak by and see if anyone was there yet, studying the signs and marks that the priest made with a soft white stick on the big black wall. They walked to the edge of the school yard, and then stood outside in the clear air, in the sun, breathing the fragrance of fresh wet snow and new bread, crusty and warm.

The singsong reciting voices floated from inside the log schoolhouse. Omakayas was glad they were outside, but Angeline's face was turned eagerly toward the sound of the priest's instructions. She was curious to know what was happening, but remembered Grandma's advice: "Take their ways if you need them," she said, "but don't forget your own. You are Anishinabe. Your mother and your grandmother are wolf clan people. Don't forget. Also, you sweat-bath yourself clean every day, even jump in the freezing lake, a thing that the chimookomanug do not do. My girl, don't become like them."

Just as the thought of Grandma made Omakayas smile, there was a flurry of stamping feet as children of all ages burst from the back door, leaping wide, flinging themselves forward in a laughing frenzy, thrilled with the prospect of new snow and ready to have their morning break, their fun, and then their small meal of smoked whitefish and bread.

"Ai! Neshkey!" Angeline pointed in amazement.

Stepping with easy care down the stairs of the school-house, solemn, carrying his tobacco pouch, his knife at his belt, was none other than Fishtail! What was he doing at the school? He did not join the children in their wild play, but walked directly from the school toward his camp. Fishtail lived at the very edge of the village, hidden in deep bush. His place was built the old way; it was a birchbark house, but it was quite warm in winter because he knew how to heap the sides with snow and he was an excellent trapper. The interior of his house was always lined with strung skins, hung with lush furs made up into sleeping robes, and red-and-white-point blankets. His wife, Angeline's best friend, Ten Snow, was known as a fine beadworker. People said that she tanned hides so soft that they felt to the skin like the slippery velvet that the traders sold.

"Let's find out what he's doing," whispered Angeline.

"He was visiting the school," said Omakayas, "what's there to find out?"

"I don't think so." Angeline pointed to the book, the sheaf of chimookoman paper, the evidence in Fishtail's hand that he had another motive in attending the school.

"Okay," said Omakayas, now curious. "You go ask him."

"Aaaaay!" Angeline blushed.

"Scared!"

"No, I'm not!"

"You are so."

Challenged, Angeline jumped forward. She walked so swiftly after Fishtail that Omakayas ran to keep up, but when she got to him she walked beside him with no word. Didn't she know what to say? Omakayas trotted behind, just within earshot.

"What were you doing back there?" Angeline finally had the courage to ask.

"I went to the priest's school. To learn to read the chimookoman's tracks. That way they can't cheat us with the treaties."

Surprised and taken aback at this, Angeline and Omakayas could only stand still and watch him as he walked swiftly, gracefully, back to his home.

They turned to go, still thoughtful. The sun was warm as summer, and by the time they returned all the snow had melted in the heat. They took the same path back they had taken before, and as they neared the cabin, all of a sudden, Omakayas felt a wet slap and a sharp, stinging blow on the back of her head. It was Pinch. Dancing with gleeful anger, foot to foot, his snowballs so watery only the pebbles are their centers were left in a pile around his feet, he nevertheless insisted on his revenge.

"I said I'd get you and I got you," he yelled. "I'm the warrior, Big Pinch!"

◄o►

Not long after that first bright snow, another snow fell, grayer and heavier. The ice came in. The water had a transparent skim that broke apart and clicked together, then went solid again, until there formed a tough gray coat of ice. Deydey surely had stopped to camp and to wait until the ice was thick before moving on. It snowed steadily and long, three days. While the snow fell outside, Angeline's friend Ten Snow used the red cloth Deydey had brought last summer as trim for a blue tradecloth dress she and Angeline were making. It was a ribbon-trimmed, graceful dress. Mama had trimmed a matching shawl with thimbles, so that when she walked Angeline jingled softly and enticingly.

Every so often now, she was allowed to visit Auntie Muskrat's house. That was the only place she was allowed to visit alone, for Auntie Muskrat kept a strict eye on her. Any young men who visited would have to stand or sit outside on Auntie's log bench while Angeline stayed, dancing foot to foot, inside the cabin, craning out the window, laughing.

The snow fell deeper yet, and in its grip Old Tallow had the best of luck. On the last day it snowed, she dragged from the farthest end of the island two plump beavers. The furs were thick and would fetch a good trade. She roped the beavers onto a little sled tied to another rope that circled her waist. Happily, she brought the meat to Mama and Grandma to prepare. She stayed in the yard, smoking her little pipe, while they made a fire outside to roast the meat over the coals.

Although snow had fallen, Omakayas thought, it couldn't be truly winter until Old Tallow put on her remarkable coat. Every year, the children watched to see that coat emerge—big and shaggy and always different, sewed with new furs, patched with discarded calicos, even velvets. Old Tallow would wear it until the earliest days of spring. But now, even though the cold already bit in the mornings, she wore only her one earth-colored dress with the raveled hem. She even looked a little too warm as she bent near the fire, pulling a burning stick out to relight the new wad of tobacco in her pipe. She leaned back, adjusting her hat, and stared long at Omakayas.

Omakayas looked into the fire. It was her job to keep smoothing and arranging the coals into an even bed for baking the meat, but Tallow's eyes on her back made her itch. Whenever Old Tallow looked at her like that, she could feel those fierce eyes resting on her skin. There was something peculiar in Old Tallow's look. Something different from the way she looked at every other human. It was something familiar, though, and this time as Omakayas glanced back and caught a corner, just a little shred of that look, she suddenly understood.

Old Tallow was looking at her the same way she looked at her dogs!

This was not a bad thing. In fact, it was good in a way, for in Old Tallow's look there was true affection, something she didn't feel for other humans. It made Omakayas feel both strange and safe inside. She smiled to herself and had the odd, sudden, curious knowledge that, if it ever came to that, Old Tallow would protect her, Omakayas, with her life.

She didn't know why she knew that, but she just knew.

Soon, Nokomis came out and took over, poking the coals this way and that to evenly set them. Soon, she would burn a fine crust onto the skin.

Beaver, or amik, was Deydey's favorite meat. He loved the burnt flavor of its fat, and Mama cooked it in a special way. As soon as the meat singed and slightly burnt, she cleaned the beavers, washed their carcasses with salted water and stuffed them with corn and potatoes. She then sewed them shut and roasted them slowly in the big iron kettle. They sizzled in their own fat and the acorns burned black. When the beavers were tender and completely cooked all through, she removed them, undid the meat from the bones, mixed the stuffing with the fried acorns and cooked it all together, in a soup, once again.

The aroma had Old Tallow pacing back and forth hungrily. She looked eager as her dogs, and when Mama ladled the soup into her bowl she bent to it with a savage will. Eating swiftly, Old Tallow put away one bowl and then another while Mama was dishing up the rest of the meal. It was lucky she ate so quickly, though, and put away so much, for just as Pinch was wiping bread, pikwayzhigun, across the bottom of his bowl and opening his mouth to ask for more, there was a stamping and shouting outside. The dogs barked, then stopped when a familiar voice shouted, "Gaygo! Gaygo!"

It was Deydey, come home.

As if summoned across the new ice by his favorite dish, he arrived in time to eat until he could eat no more. That night, the children went upstairs and slept in the loft, and Nokomis slept there, too, instead of downstairs beside Mama. Nokomis made her bed at the farthest end of the loft, where it was coolest. She put her old rabbit-skin blanket down and slept on top of it.

"I sleep hot," she explained to the children.

They didn't like to tell her, but she also slept noisy. Nokomis snored and often talked in her sleep, calling out to people from long ago. That night, Omakayas woke in the dark and listened to her grandmother's soft regular breathing and then her murmur, half understandable, sometimes arguing and sometimes pleasant as she dreamed old times and went visiting to places that only she remembered.

Biboon

(WINTER)

CHAPTER NINE

The Blue Ferns

 NOW FILLED THE world, falling deeper and deeper, changing the island. The cabin was made in the chimookoman way. Deydey was proud of its snug construction, with thick logs fitted together as closely as possible. The heaviest mud he could find, the stickiest clay, Deydey tamped between the logs to seal the cracks. He'd put cross-beams up top and split logs to make a tiny loft where Omakayas, Angeline, and Pinch slept on their woven reed mats placed over tufts of moss.

Grandma still slept at the coldest end of the loft, only now in her thick rabbit-fur blanket. Cold crept along the floor. Omakayas was glad of the boring time she'd spent over the summer pressing fistfuls of gumbo clay, taken from the center of the island, into those places where the dried mud had crumbled. The warmest places in the house were on the sides she had mended best. Cold air sneaked in just where she'd run out of muck and had to use grass. Sometimes, the wind whistled when it entered. That thin whine sent a shiver down her back.

Now that Deydey was home, the cabin changed, too. Filled with his traps and blankets, his big man's coat and head wrap, his moose-hide mitts and traveling kettles, ice chisels, ax, his makazins old again within Mama's embrace, and his new gun secure on pegs over the door, the cabin seemed smaller, cozier, in a way more interesting, Omakayas thought.

And more difficult, too.

People stopped in at any time of day or even in the deep of night, and these visitors required constant attention. Yellow Kettle and Grandma were known as the keepers of a good store of food and a warm fire, although Omakayas, Angeline, and Pinch were the ones responsible for hauling the water for tea and chopping the wood for the fire that burned in the proud little hearth. The fires needed constant vigilance, as did family needs. Deydey's gun required his concentrated care, and he liked tea at his elbow while he cleaned the workings and barrel.

It seemed to Omakayas that every time the grown-ups began to talk, they discussed travel routes west. They argued whether the pressure of so many newcomers was going to send them the way so many others were sent, into the territory of the Bwaanug, the Dakota. There was now constant talk of government intentions, plans to meet in council, invitations to smoke the pipe. At least there were less serious visitors, including Two Strike Girl, Wishkob and Auntie Muskrat, Twilight and Little Bee. Angeline's favorite friend, young Ten Snow, came by to visit almost every day. Albert LaPautre came early to tell his dreams to Deydey, who tried to take them seriously.

"Last night I dreamed my head got stuck in a kettle," he revealed, his voice low and troubled.

"It must have been a very big kettle," Deydey said, solemnly, for LaPautre had a big round head and a full moon face.

"Geget," said LaPautre. He never understood teasing jokes. "It *was* big. Even so, what does it mean?"

"Some dreams are so powerful they are beyond our humble ability to comprehend," said Deydey.

LaPautre leaned back, satisfied. Only Mama caught Deydey's wink.

Even Old Tallow stopped over to eat whatever she was given, often standing outside the door and bolting soup before she hurried off to hunt.

And, yes, she had now donned her coat!

The coat of Old Tallow was a fantastic thing, woven of various pelts, including one of lynx, one of beaver, a deer hide, and two that belonged to beloved dogs. She had pieced together old blankets, one a faded red, one brown. Discarded shreds of unidentifiable stuffs were sewed patch on patch, including some black beaded velvets and bright calicos. The coat fit across her in a great mound, and flapped when she moved. She wore it well, springing lightly along like a huge, tattered bear.

No cold seemed to bother Old Tallow, but if it was too biting a day to walk outside or slide on the ice, Ten Snow and Angeline sat in the corner of the cabin on bedrolls and piles of skins. There, light from the window of thick oiled paper falling golden on their faces, the two young women sewed and talked. Ten Snow had finished something very impressive, much admired by the other women, including Grandma, who took it in her hands and blessed it one cold day. It was a bag for Fishtail, a fashionable bandolier bag. Instead of the dyed quills Grandma used so skillfully, Ten Snow had sewn the bag with trade beads bought in precious

packets at the company store. The bag was covered with four beaver-skins' worth of white beads—they were expensive! Fishtail's square bag was beaded all over in swirls of green vines, leaves, and glowing crimson flowers that popped out vividly against the white beads of the backround. The shoulder strap, too, was entirely beaded. The strap's design was simple, unusual, and consisted of blue curls that Ten Snow bashfully explained were the uncoiled heads of new spring ferns, her husband's favorite food. Looking at it, Omakayas had to blink her eyes, for the beads were so perfect and the repeated pattern so compelling that the ferns seemed to move like little waves.

"Will you teach me how to bead that pattern?" Angeline asked her friend.

"Ayah!" Ten Snow removed from her little sewing kit a needle, and Angeline took out her own work, her own beads, bought with dried whitefish. They began.

"Gayay neen," said Omakayas, "me, too!" Ten Snow smiled gently, and Angeline looked at her little sister in surprise.

"You?" She grinned. "Little Frog, little jumper, can you sit still that long?"

Stung by her sister's amused tone of voice, Omakayas dropped her head to her chest, eyes squinting narrow. A huge space opened up in her head, black and rushing as a freezing winter stream. She was old enough to tan the stinking old hides, wasn't she? Her work was valued there, wasn't it? Why shouldn't she be trusted to use the precious beads? She was eight winters now! She wasn't that little! She could chop wood, haul the water from the hole Nokomis kept open in the ice with an ax and a long, sharp pole. Why couldn't she bead like the older girls?

Angeline laughed out loud. Omakayas turned away. Her heart shrunk cold in her chest, tiny but heavy as a lake rock. How her sister's words could stab her sometimes! But now, as though she hadn't noticed Angeline's remark at all, Ten Snow's hand was stroking Omakayas's arm and she was speaking.

"Sssshhhh, ishte, Little Sister, I made something for you."

Into Omakayas's hands she placed a small leather packet. Omakayas looked up at Ten Snow, uncertain.

"Yes, for you." Ten Snow gestured for her to open it and slowly, with unbelieving delight, Omakayas did. The leather packet was lined with broadcloth and into the cloth two needles were stuck. Two! Around a peeled twig Ten Snow had wound a long length of the finest sinew thread to use in beading. At the end of the cloth, a small pocket held a lump of fragrant, summery yellow bees-wax to use in strengthening the sinew thread. And best of all, she saw, as Ten Snow lifted up the dark blue strip of cloth, there was a tiny sack of all colors of beads, seed beads, the little grown-up kind of beads, shining and gleaming against the cloth.

Manidominenz, they were called. Little spirit seeds.

"Megwetch, megwetch, megwetch!" Omakayas thanked Ten Snow over and over again until the older girl couldn't help smiling. The youngest of her family, Ten Snow had no little sisters and, as yet, no children. So she was extra-kind to Omakayas. As the older girls returned to their work and their talk, Omakayas curled near the fire to look at her beads and to imagine what she would make with them. At first, she thought that she might bead some tiny makazins for her dolls. Then she thought Angeline might make fun of her project. Mama, something for Mama? She had so many quilled things, and preferred them. Besides, Grandma was always making a box or an ornament for her. How about for Grandma, for Deydey, for Angeline? Certainly not for Pinch, who would spoil anything he got. Or Neewo, who might chew off the beads.

Neewo. Suddenly, she knew, as though the beads told her themselves, that they were meant for her little brother. Omakayas would make something very special for him—she saw what she would make coming clear. Makazins! Warm makazins, trimmed with rabbit fur. In her mind, she planned them out, sewn from scraps of moosehide that were left over from the summer. She saw them with white flowers beaded on the ankles, woolen balls of blanket thread to decorate the cuffs. Admiring her idea, gloating, planning, Omakayas turned the leather sewing kit and bead packet over and over in her hands.

Mama and Grandma set their work out on blankets before them. Grandma was completing the edge of a great round box of birchbark, one that she would use to store her red willow kinnikinnick. She was binding the edges with strips of basswood bark and sinew. She had cut fancy shapes of stars out to sew on the sides. Mama had set aside Deydey's fancy moose-hide coat jacket in order to finish Angeline's fine clothing to wear at the gathering dance that would be held as soon as a few more families had set up their winter households.

Grandma, meanwhile, had finished a beautiful dance fan made of a partridge tail. Its handle was birchbark, bound tightly, quilled with sweet flowers.

The thimbles that Mama was sewing onto Angeline's shawl caught orange sparks of fire as Mama worked each one onto the wide strip of ribbon. First she punched a little hole in the tip of the thimble with her awl, then she threaded a bit of red cord through, knotted the end well inside the thimble, and sewed the end of the cord underneath the ribbon so it didn't show. As soon as she took the last stitch, Angeline clapped her hands.

"Let me try it on!" cried Angeline, impatiently.

Laughing, Mama handed it to her, and beautiful Angeline wrapped herself in its fine swirl. Grandma handed her the dance fan. Everyone admired.

"Mama," said Omakayas, "can you help me now?"

"Ayah, geget," Mama said.

They left off looking at Angeline, and started work on Neewo's makazins. From the moose hide left over from Deydey's makazins, Mama helped Omakayas cut out a pair of makazins for Neewo, winter makazins with cuffs well up his legs for warmth. Omakayas planned out a flower and began immediately, imitating Mama, to sew the beads into the design. It was harder, more exacting work than she thought. The sinew tangled and knotted. Beads bounced off the needle's tip. Even when she fastened the beads on, sometimes they looked odd or crooked, and she had to take them off. She put her needle down. Tears of frustration stung.

"Don't give up." It was Angeline, her voice gentle, kind. "You are doing very well, neshemay, little sister."

Omakayas looked at her big sister in surprise, then gratitude. Nothing felt as good as this unexpected kindness from Angeline. She wiped her tears away, and took up her beadwork again.

Neewo was napping in his little blanket hammock just above them. Deydey had tied two ropes into holes in

the wooden beams, and between the two he'd fastened a warm blanket into a hammock. Mama could rock Neewo by moving her foot, tied to one of the ropes, or Omakayas could swing him by moving the other end of a rope.

The sky darkened. Pinch was sent out to bring wood. He made a face at Omakayas, for with her bead-work she was set apart, another of the women, and Pinch was left to fetch wood all by himself. Deydey and Fishtail sat in the corner, talking low and thoughtfully, drinking Grandma's tea. Soon they got up and left, for they had decided to try their luck with the fishing nets let down through big holes chopped in the ice. They went out the door, talking louder the minute they were outside. There was a little space of quiet around the women, all together. The time seemed just right to ask Nokomis for a story.

"Weendamawashin, daga, Nokomis," Omakayas asked. "Tell me a story."

"What story do you want to hear?"

"Windigo!" said Pinch, returning, his arms stacked with wood.

"Are you sure you want to hear it?" Nokomis growled deep in her chest, showed her sharp teeth.

"Owah!" Pinch's eyes rounded, but his grin was full

of excitement. He inched closer to Nokomis and tried to shush baby Neewo, who had awakened. Neewo could wiggle out of his cradleboard now, at last, and was learning to walk. He pulled himself along by grasping shoulders, clothes, hair, anything to keep upright. When eventually he plumped down, he showed his pleasure by trying to bang his stick doll to pieces against the side of the hearth.

"Gaygo," Omakayas said, but her voice was gentle as she showed Neewo how to dance the doll instead of break it.

"Pinch!"

From outside, the men were calling him. The big men! He clattered down the wood, jumped to his feet, and ran out the door. Being called by the men was better than a story, even a windigo story, any old day.

Once again, the women and Neewo were left alone.

"Now," Nokomis said, "I can tell you an old story about my grandmother." She looked tellingly at Mama. "You know the one."

"Geget," said Mama, only half-teasingly. "Do you think they're old enough to hear it?"

"I was eight winters old when it happened," said Grandma. "Same as Omakayas now."

"Then tell it," Omakayas begged.

"Yes, tell it," said Angeline.

Ten Snow put down her work for a moment to beg, laughingly, along with everyone else.

GRANDMA'S STORY

◄O►

Fishing the Dark Side
of the Lake

When I was just a little girl, said Nokomis, her voice lilting high, and dropping low, her voice far away, I was told by my grandfather, who I lived with, who raised me, never to fish the dark side of the lake.

Why, you wonder? I never knew that either. Never found out until, of course, being a young girl and very curious, I took my grandfather's canoe out one day while he was sleeping. I put my fishing spear and nets in the canoe. I would fish where the water was deepest, strangest, bluest on clear days and blackest on the cloudy days. That's where I paddled. I had a stick and line. I let that down, baited, and I waited to see what sort of fish I would catch.

The wait was long, my grandchildren, and as I fished there I grew uneasy. I remembered my grandfa-

ther's warnings, the way he insisted that I was never to approach this deep water. I'd seen him looking out there, sometimes at sunset, his eyes sad and clear. Sometimes he mentioned my grandmother. She had gone away young, I knew that. Not much more. Her favorite food, he said, was fresh plums. She could stand beneath a plum tree and eat all day, he said. When he said that, he smiled.

Fresh wild plums. I had taken dark red plums with me. As I sat in the boat waiting for the fish to bite, I put them slowly, one by one, into my mouth. What was wrong with this side of the lake? I had to wonder. Except for the depth and darkness, it wasn't much different. I would find out what was different, I decided. I kept my line in the water.

My bait must have been wrong, though. My bait must have been no good. I didn't get a bite, even a little nibble. Maybe, I thought, Grandfather told me not to fish this dark side of the lake because no fish lived here! That would be a joke on me! Just then, I looked over the side of the boat and I spilled all the rest of my plums into the water. Saaa! I was disgusted. Down they went, to the bottom. Not long after they sank from sight, though, I had a strong tug on my line. Then not just a tug, a real pull. Soon I was struggling to keep from being dragged overboard. I had caught something. Something very huge!

A hand reached out of the water! Pulled itself up my fishing line, finger over finger, fist over fist, until suddenly the beautiful face of a woman appeared. She looked up at me and kept climbing.

"Do you have more plums?" she asked.

I said no, but I helped her into the boat anyway. Her hair was black and endlessly long, covering her, and underneath it she was naked. Her smile was gentle. Her skin was purple, gray, cold, the color of those plums. There was something familiar about her, something awful and yet famil-iar. I was very much afraid and began to paddle quickly back to Grandfather.

Still, I was a curious child.

"Who are you?" I asked as we traveled along.

"I am your grandmother," she said, "here's what happened. Long ago, I married your grandfather. We could not be parted. We were like one person, he and I. He was stingy with me. After I bore our first child and lay her in his arms, after she grew for a year, I became my daring self again. I became again the wild girl he'd loved from the beginning. One night, I dared him to swim with me in the lake. We went out in our canoe to the deepest part of the lake, the darkest and the coldest side, where you have found me. We threw off our clothing. I dived in deep as I could, pulled my way down, down, until I reached the bottom.

"My dear grandchild, that's when I got lost. It was so dark down at the bottom that I got turned around. I could not find my way back up again, and so, tired, I curled up in the cold weeds and I went to sleep. Until now."

My grandmother looked toward the shore. Her face glowed in the twilight. I saw, as we approached, that she was watching my grandfather as he came down the path from the camp to the edge of the lake. He walked closer, closer. Something strange happened. I rubbed my eyes. I passed my hand across my face.

I could not believe what I was seeing.

As he approached, my grandfather's step seemed to pick up life. His hair got darker and darker until it turned the pure black of his youth. Lines disappeared from his face. He straightened his bowed back. Just as our canoe touched the shore, he smiled. And oh, my grandchildren, suddenly he had all of his teeth!

I got out of the canoe. He looked upon me kindly,

said good-bye to me, and then he took my place in the canoe with his young wife. The two gazed into each other's faces with great happiness. I watched the two paddle away together, into the darkness, into the night. Two shooting stars passed over through the sky. The lake was silent. I never again saw my grandfather, but eventually his clothing was found on the shore, washed up on the dark side of the lake.

—<o>—

When Nokomis finished, no word was spoken. Omakayas could say nothing because stiff hairs prickled at the back of her neck. She couldn't get the sight of that hand, reaching out of the water, from her mind! Ten Snow and Angeline were wiping tears from their eyes. Mama sighed and continued her work, slowly, carefully, on Angeline's shawl. Perhaps she was thinking of the big gathering, where Angeline might meet someone and go away with him, far from her mother's gaze. Although she didn't want that to happen, it was inevitable, and Yellow Kettle's fond look said all that was in her heart. How deeply she loved her children. How dear they were to her, the center of her life. Being naturally cheerful and bold, though, she soon grinned and joked. Yellow Kettle could not help turning the mood her way and soon everyone was laughing over Neewo's tumbling and Andeg's playful squawks as Neewo followed him, grabbed for him. Andeg knew how to stay just out of reach of those chubby, curious fingers!

CHAPTER TEN

The Visitor

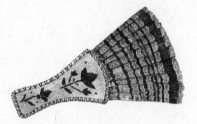

 FIRE WAS KINDLED in the center of the dance lodge, and its fragrant smoke rose through the central opening in the roof. The fire was hardly needed though, in spite of the cold, for the crowd of dancers, the drummers, the children, the old men in the farthest corner gambling, seated on soft skins, the old ladies at their games and gossip, the young women in the center and the young men surrounding them, the people of all ages talking, laughing, and dancing, kept the great lodge warm.

Omakayas loved the drum. The beat throbbed through her, drumming her entirely alive and eager. The soles of her feet tingled. Her hands moved in time to the song. Angeline danced, too, wearing her new shawl and holding Grandma's partridge-tail fan. Standing at the center with Ten Snow, she gracefully bounced to the beat. Thimbles ringing, her body moved in exact time. Mama, when she was only known as that swift girl Yellow Kettle and had no children, had always loved to dance. She bobbed in the corner, contented and proud of her daughters, Neewo alongside her. Even Nokomis couldn't help dancing. Omakayas stopped to watch her grandmother step along with such care and dignity she seemed to be crossing a rushing stream on small stones. Her steps were small and light as a deer's, Omakayas thought, watching her proudly.

Heat radiated from the fire, and the faces of the girls and young women turned rosy-red and warm. Trade silver tokens, bracelets, armbands, crosses flashed and ribbons swirled as the dancers moved in joy and excitement, crying out for another song as soon as each was done. The drum intensified, the laughter turned ever more hilarious. The old men won and lost in their makazin gambling game, and the children wove in and out of the movement, hiding from one another, tagging around the side of a parent, teasing and sometimes dancing, too. Around the middle of the night, everybody stopped to partake of the feast—a big kettle of venison and corn soup was brought in by the fire and children were sent back to houses and lodges for birchbark makuks and tin bowls.

While they were eating, teasing, commenting on the soup, flavored with low-growing juniper berries and parched hot summer corn, something happened that disturbed everyone and changed the course of the winter. Indeed, what happened changed the way Omakayas and her family lived from then on. A visitor entered. He and his voyageur crew had just dragged their sled of furs across from the mainland, and were staying for the night. Thinking back, Omakayas could even remember him, sitting by the fire as close as he could without scorching, a tired-looking man, thin and scraggly braids, coughing and feeble. A bit confused-looking. A flushed, fevered face. It was hearing of his death in hushed tones, though, the next day, that she would always recall. The report of it. For the horror flooded swiftly from house to house, lodge to lodge.

He died of smallpox.

Although the visitor's body was taken to the farthest end of the island, although everything he'd touched was burned, including the lodge he'd stayed in and the blankets he wore, although the generous family who let him in purified themselves in the sweat lodge, burned all of their belongings, and threw themselves upon the mercy of the mission, fear abounded in the settlement. Had the visitor left another, more horrible visitor behind? Sickness? Death?

Angeline's face was taut with worry. She knew that her kind Ten Snow, noticing the stranger's discomfort, had put her own bowl, filled with soup, into his hands. She then brought that bowl back to the lodge she shared with Fishtail, and although that bark onagun was thrown far away and buried now in snow, there was no knowing whether it would bring down the disease and its evils.

During the next few days everyone watched carefully for any signs of the sickness. And signs soon came. Ten Snow was the first to fall into a fever, and then those in the lodge where the sick man had stayed fell ill, one after the next. The entire family down to the oldest grandfather and the tiniest baby suffered in the helpless hands of missionaries, who closed the school and kept them fed and warm on the floors of the building, just below the blackboard where Fishtail had finally learned to write his chimookoman name.

Six days later, just when Mama and Nokomis were hoping that the scratching sickness had passed them over, Angeline did not rise from her blankets. Overnight, the fever had seized her and she lay hot and stifled, face red, eyes wild with fear when Mama came up to check on her. Omakayas came, too, behind Mama, but with a stern look Mama sent her back down the ladder.

"Take care of Pinch and Neewo. Keep them downstairs," she ordered. Her voice, as she called Deydey and looked over the edge of the loft, was calm with despair.

"Build a bark lodge outside, good and warm," she instructed. "Nokomis will take care of the children. You stay out there, too."

And so, by the end of the day, the little family was divided. Inside the house, supplied with firewood and water, Mama and Angeline battled the invisible enemy. Outside, the others slept heavily and fearfully in the lodge made from rolls of bark saved in the lean-to. Neewo curled with Omakayas around the tiny lodge fire. Pinch huddled next to Nokomis. Deydey slept alone.

On the third day, the evil day, Mama did not appear at the door to bring in the water Deydey fetched. Nokomis went in and did not return for a long time. When she did show her face, she called from the doorway to Deydey.

"My daughter has the sickness along with Angeline. Keep the children warm. Feed them good."

She then disappeared into the cabin, and Deydey

spent the day chopping wood, hauling water, hunting, and talking to Old Tallow, who had come near in grim worry. The two sat hunched over the fire for a long while, drinking cups of strong swamp tea. Finally, Tallow lifted her gun, looped her rabbit snares around her wrists and set out to hunt, now with more urgency than ever. On the eighth day, Pinch fell sick and was moved into the cabin where Nokomis took care of them all. Outside, Deydey worked continually, emptying pots from inside and chopping holes in ice, fishing to keep them strong, making sure the water in their kettle was always fresh and clear, their wood piled high.

Higher. Higher.

"Why are you continuing to pile up the wood?" Omakayas asked him, fearful, watching how he sweated and labored at the woodpile. "Rest, Deydey," she begged, in fear at his fixed and set face, his deep eyes. He gave her a look of annoyance, as though from far away, and then, seeing that she offered him a cup of rabbit soup, seeing that her face was chilled with terror for him, he softened.

"Gaween, my little frog," he said, pausing, his voice unusually gentle. "I cannot stop. I want to get a lot of wood ahead so I can take a little rest, eh?"

He smiled at her, but his smile was weary. The

gentle exhaustion in his voice terrified her more than anything that had happened so far. That night she lay sleepless, gazing at the flickering of the flames on the ceiling, wondering what was happening inside the cabin, listening to her father's even breathing and Neewo's tiny, rumbling snore. It was as though the sickness was sucking first one, then the next, and the next, into the cabin—where they disappeared and did not emerge. How could Nokomis care for them all? What if Deydey got sick, too? Somehow, it never occurred to her that she or Neewo could sicken. Deydey was the one she watched carefully. Not Neewo. It was as though her little brother were part of her, she kept him so near. She didn't understand at all when Neewo fell ill.

Or maybe she couldn't let the fact in, because she just loved her little brother so much. Maybe that.

It happened in the night, as she held him close. Omakayas felt his small body turn heated and molten, soft and fiery with the fever's rage. He was red, quiet, and limp in her arms when Deydey woke, and Omakayas held him close, gently bathed his face with a bit of snow, hoping that he would grin at her, hoping that again he would be healthy and sweet. She didn't want the house, the sickness, to suck him in, too. It couldn't! She wouldn't let it! But as soon as she dozed off, Deydey lifted little Neewo away. She woke immediately, crawled to the door of the lodge, and then, as Deydey walked toward the silent cabin with the tiniest thread of smoke coming from the chimney, Omakayas saw him stagger. He didn't fall, but she knew from that misstep that Deydey was ill, that he'd hidden his sickness, and that he was going into the cabin with Neewo, never to return.

Omakayas acted without hesitation. She put out the little fire in the birchbark house.

If they were all to die together, then let it be so. She would not stay outside alone and away from those she loved, no, not even if it meant her life. She followed Neewo inside.

◄○►

The air in the cabin was thick with the stink of disease, but the hearth was warm. Nokomis had the sick ones arranged in their bedding, blankets pulled neatly up to their chins, mats clean on the floor all around the fire. Although Nokomis sat next to Mama in a stupor of exhaustion and did not at first speak to Omakayas, she nodded encouragingly at Angeline, who slept easily now, her fever broken, her hands limp on her blanket. Omakayas crouched beside her. That's when she saw that the beautiful face of her sister was covered with ugly sores and vivid lumps, and her mouth, when she opened it to breathe, showed that her gums bled painfully and stained her teeth red. Her hair was caught in a thick mat, but she was alive. Her breath moved steadily, in and out.

Mama slept, also covered with sores, unconscious and still in the depth of her danger. Pinch kept tossing off his covers or dragging at Mama's. With a weary, loving, unthinking movement that showed she had done this thousands of times before, Nokomis replaced the blankets. Held a tin cup of water to Pinch's lips. Trickled a little water between Mama's lips, then Angeline's. Deydey, slumped over by the fire, she did not disturb except to lower him to the earth. Motioning to Omakayas, she indicated Neewo, who was trembling now, his tiny arms and legs moving jerkily as the heat in his body increased, and increased, until he had not the strength to even cry.

"Keep holding him," said Nokomis tenderly, giving Neewo to Omakayas, seating them by the fire. She placed her dry, old, cool hand on the back of Omakayas's head. "Just keep holding him," she said again.

And so Omakayas did. She held Neewo through the night, dozing with him, waking when he thrashed, cleaning him, bathing with cool water his forehead and his tiny, straining, bony chest. His clenched hands and his beautiful feet. She held him when he melted into a troubled sleep. When his breath rasped. When his cough deepened. When he cried and cried until his voice was gone. She held him when he grew still and quiet, too quiet. When his fever came back.

One day passed, another blurred, and still she held her little brother. Held him close in her arms. She held him as he looked mysteriously into her face, his eyes huge. She held him when he spat up blood. When he whimpered for Andeg, who sat high up in the roof beams, head underneath his wing. She held him through another night, held him when his chest went drum-tight and he struggled for breath. Held him when he drew that breath, deep from the heart.

She held him when he died.

She held him close. She didn't know exactly when his life went except that Andeg croaked three times, longingly, as though for his playmate. Then, Omakayas knew that something had changed. Her little brother's body no longer warmed her with its heat, they were the same temperature and then he was colder. Still, she did not let him go. Nokomis had to take him from her arms, and when she did Omakayas fell down on the blanket, arms still held in the cradle shape of her brother, and knew nothing all that day.

It was night when she woke.

Opening her eyes, she knew at once what had happened and the bleak knowledge made her shut her eyes again. Maybe, almost, she wished that she were sick, too, that she could join him. For Nokomis had said that the Ojibwa must walk a path that leads out of this life into the next, and since Neewo couldn't walk very well yet, who would carry him when he got tired, when he fell? Who would make sure he was fed in the other world? Who would make him toy man dolls to dance? Who would care for him when he was lost?

The answer, once she had risen, once she began working with Nokomis to care for her family, was a sad answer. Old Tallow brought the news later that day. She set four snared rabbits down near the door, then waited to speak.

"Ten Snow is gone," she said.

On the road to the next world, surely, she and Neewo would meet, thought Omakayas, tears blinding her as she tipped water to her father's lips. Surely Ten Snow would take hold of Neewo's hand, swing him up in her arms, carry him along past the rough spots and danger, to the place where they would be safe.

Old Tallow took the horn spoon from Omakayas and ordered her to lie down, to sleep. She made Nokomis lie down as well in the corner, with her grandchild.

"You two rest now! Go on or I'll take a stick to you!" Her voice was fierce, rasping, angry, and strong. Nokomis obeyed her, sank into the skins, slept before her head touched the back of her blanket.

Omakayas was glad to do the same.

Old Tallow then proceeded to work. She built up the fire, high, to a greater heat than Nokomis had dared, for she knew she could chop more wood as needed. She brought a new kettle of water in, skinned her rabbits by the light of the fire and boiled them for a nourishing soup. She cleaned every corner, the way she never cleaned her own house. She left her dogs to run wild and tended every need, cared for the humans she loved and, although she never would admit it, loved even more than she loved her dogs.

Old Tallow's work helped them, but the next day she left once more to hunt. Nokomis weakened, though she wasn't ill. Omakayas alone was left to tend to the sick ones. She had to keep the fire going, haul the water, cover them, bathe them down, comfort them when they were restless. She hardly slept an hour at a time. First one needed her, then the other. Then a third, the first again. There was no stopping. Their cries were pitiful.

When the terrible itching that gave the disease its

name started, Omakayas wrapped their hands with cloth, bit down their fingernails, anything to keep them from scarring themselves. The itching nearly drove them from their minds. Pinch was worst, and he'd weakened so badly that Nokomis was afraid for him. Night and day, one or the other sat with him and did not let go of his hand for fear he would run to the land of the spirits. Even Andeg seemed to sense how close Pinch was to death. Andeg perched near Pinch, as though keeping guard. Every time Pinch slipped too far away the bird croaked, "Gaygo, Pinch!" One stubborn eye flared open and Pinch fixed his annoyed little boy glare upon the bird. He was mad, but he got well. "Gaygo Pinch! Gaygo! Gaygo!" called Andeg. What he really meant was *Don't go! Stay here!*

One night, Omakayas woke to see Deydey trying to rise to his feet. In the dim light of a low fire, she saw him throw off his blankets. He tried to stagger outside. She knew that was certain death. Many died of this sickness when they became so fevered that they lost their minds, threw off blankets, and walked outside to freeze.

"Please, Deydey," she said, to draw him back.

He sank onto all fours, but kept crawling determinedly toward the door, groaning, hair wild. His eyes did not know her and his face was frightful. He clawed at the door, fell to his knees. Got up on his knees. This time, he was so determined that Omakayas knew there was no way she could save him from going outside. He was too strong for her, even in his sickness.

"Gaween onjidah," she said, "I'm sorry."

Raising a block of wood high, she brought it down on his head with all of her strength. He crumpled to the ground. Omakayas sobbed as she dragged his blankets to him and covered him. He was too heavy to drag near the fire. For a long time she kneeled next to him, praying for him to live. She loved him, her Deydey. What would they do without him? Back in her own blankets, she immediately sank into a fierce oblivion. When she woke, it was morning. Instantly, she remembered the night before.

Was her father dead? Had her blow killed him? Fear gripped her as she crept to his side, put her hand to his lips. His breath came evenly. He seemed a little better, even, than the day before. As the morning went on he sipped broth for the first time. Opened his eyes.

"My little frog." He smiled, closing his eyes again, this time to sleep comfortably. "You could bring down a bear with the strength in your club." His fever was broken at last.

Omakayas's constant attention brought the little family through the first part of the illness's danger. One by one, they improved, all because of her careful nursing. Later, it was the vaccine of the Reverend Hall, fetched from the mainland, that guarded the rest of the Ojibwa who had been exposed and who survived the smallpox of 1847. Eighteen Ojibwa died of the disease, and one tried to kill himself by other means.

That man was Fishtail. No one had understood it of him, but his wife was everything. When Ten Snow left him, Fishtail would not leave her body. He slashed his arms and was found in the blanket beside her, half alive. He survived. But once he had the strength, he cut off his long, thick, splendid hair. He buried it with the sweet woman who was called Ten Snow not because her own skin was white, nor because she had much of anything to do with snow at all, but because the kind assurance of her nature had reminded her namers of the way the deep snow covers and forgives all it touches when it falls.

⊰○⊱

In the deep of winter, Neewo and Ten Snow were buried side by side. A great bonfire was lighted in order to thaw the ground. Neewo and Ten Snow were wrapped in red blankets, then birchbark, and at last laid gently into their good mother, Akeeng, the earth. As soon as Deydey was better, he and Fishtail worked side by side constructing the grave houses for their loved ones. At the western end of each little house, they carefully framed a small windowlike opening, and built beneath it a shelf for spirit offerings. Although food was scarce, Mama often brought Neewo a little something saved from her own bowl and placed it on the shelf with tobacco.

She stayed long in the cold, wrapped in her blanket, praying for her little boy. At the burying ground, there were many new graves. The winter was hard. As she sat talking to her child's spirit, someone else almost always came near, added their tobacco, said a few words of comfort, and passed on to their own grieving.

Omakayas got sick, too, but not with the smallpox.

A wholly different fever followed upon her family's recovery, an illness of weakness and grief. Even as her mother strengthened and her father got better and became more and more himself, Omakayas retreated from the world. She ate less and less, thought long into the night. Often, in her mind's eye, she saw Neewo's tiny makazins, forlorn in the firelight, as they sagged, tipped over when in his fever he kicked them off. He never wore them again in his short life.

Her brother Pinch, however, more than recovered. From the loft, she could hear him downstairs, ruder and louder than ever. She heard her bird, Andeg, scratching on the floor. She heard Old Tallow come and go. She heard her grandmother, singing an old song as she stirred something fragrant in the kettle. Gently Mama called her from the base of the ladder. She heard this, but Omakayas kept her eyes closed.

Food did not interest her. All she did was think of Neewo. She considered what she could have done to arrest the illness. Fed him more soup? Forced him to keep his makazins warm on his feet? Taken him out, away, into the woods? There lived alone with him until the smallpox had run its course? And Mama, Omakayas worried about her, too. She was so quiet and thin, so restrained. When she sat, she didn't just sit still, it was like she turned to stone. In her eyes there was such a deep and penetrating look of loss that Omakayas could not bear to see her at all. Angeline was some comfort, though still weak. She kept badgering Old Tallow to bring her a mirror, but the old woman refused until one day Angeline screamed at her, shockingly, that she wanted to see herself. "Am I so bad-looking?" she yelled in rage. "Am I so ugly now?"

"Gaween," said Old Tallow, very slowly, the lines in her face shadowing, "you are still beautiful."

Omakayas, lying next to her sister, closed her eyes in pain. The smallpox had left Angeline's cheeks pitted with scars and slightly twisted Angeline's perfect hunting bow of a dark mouth. The smallpox had thinned her face until her teeth stuck out. The smallpox, worst of all, had killed Angeline's tiny brother and the friend of her heart, Ten Snow. Pain and loss showed in deep furrows around her sister's mouth.

The mirror came, a scrap of it anyway, and Angeline stared into it. Slowly, her eyes filled. When she had seen enough, she put the mirror down gently, turned away, and refused for a long time to speak.

◄◦►

It was difficult for Omakayas to understand all that had happened. Why Neewo was gone, though at night she still imagined that she heard his cries. Why her sister's face would never again be smooth. Why she herself was still too weak to run and crept back to her sleeping blanket whenever she could. She slept and slept as though she would never wake. She didn't want to think about the things that had happened, but there were times that questions came to her, occurring in the deep of night, sometimes even in dreams.

The spirits, the manitous who lived in all things, why had they ignored her prayers, her mother's prayers, and the powerful prayers of Nokomis? Why had Deydey's strength not helped? And her grandmother's medicine, so useful at other times, why hadn't it worked for Neewo? Nokomis said, sorrowfully, that she had no medicines for this white man's disease. But Omakayas did not have smallpox. Omakayas had something else. Why didn't the strong tea made of bitter bark, the tea that Nokomis brewed for Omakayas, send her jumping up lively as she used to be?

Sometimes she thought that if only her mother would laugh, she also would begin to feel better. But

Yellow Kettle was dull and angry with sorrow, and couldn't help her own daughter. Day after day passed, and Nokomis's teas grew more bitter. She made a stronger concoction, burned sweetgrass braids, fanned Omakayas, too, but the deep cold seemed to have seized her heart. She was ashamed of the way she thought sometimes, up in her blanket. Listening to Pinch, her annoying brother, who didn't seem sad at all, she wondered why Neewo was taken and Pinch left behind. Why was Neewo taken to the next world and *she* left behind? There was no explanation that satisfied her. Nothing that gave her the hope she needed to rise and take up the rest of her life. Not even when Angeline bravely smashed the little piece of mirror one day and left the cabin, walking out the door, determined to go to the missionary school and learn the meaning of the white man's writing, like Fishtail, not even then was Omakayas inspired to come downstairs.

Nokomis sat with her, quilling, through the whole day sometimes. She told her old stories, adventures of Nanabozho, the tricky and generous teacher of the Anishinabeg, who cleverly outwitted dangerous foes and taught the Anishinabeg to survive. Omakayas listened, but did not find in the stories the will to go forward. Could Nanabozho have outwitted smallpox? Could

Nanabozho push back the dreadful day, send home the awful visitor who had taken Neewo and Ten Snow? Could Nanabozho at least say a word or two in his own defense, or encourage Omakayas to go on with her life? Nothing happened. No voices explained things. Her dreams were blank.

One day, however, Old Tallow unexpectedly appeared at the top of the ladder. In her rough, steady hand she held a bark container of rabbit soup boiled up with potatoes from the storage cache. "Eat this," she urged Omakayas. "Or else!" she threatened when Omakayas was reluctant. After Omakayas had taken the first taste, Tallow insisted that she drink until she couldn't fit in another drop.

"Ah, there," said Tallow, approvingly. "You need to get your strength back."

Omakayas nodded and closed her eyes.

"Don't sleep now," said Tallow gruffly, "the sky is clear. Your brother is sliding on the lake. Go out. Be childish."

Omakayas kept her eyes closed and lengthened her breath, hoping that Old Tallow would believe that she had fallen asleep. After a while, the old woman fell silent, though she continued to sit near Omakayas, pondering what she should do next. Of course, she was suspicious.

Omakayas felt Tallow's gaze locked on her. After all, she was a hunter used to waiting at the dens of animals. If anyone could find a way to surprise Omakayas back to life, it would be her. Omakayas determined to outwait her, to crawl deeper and deeper into her dark burrow of sleep. Eventually, as though from far away, Omakayas felt the tentative brush of Tallow's tough, creased palm, and heard the rustle of her clothes as she got up and quietly left.

At first, Omakayas tried to think she had won, that she had outwitted Old Tallow and made her impatient, as even the wariest animals often failed to do. But then the time stretched long. Omakayas couldn't sleep. Her feet tingled to run. Energy from the rabbit soup flowed through her and she drummed her fingers against the floor. She was stubborn, shut her eyes. Who was fooling whom? she wondered. The sun was shining brilliantly outside. Had she really bested Old Tallow, and at whose expense? None other than her own. With a sigh, Omakayas got up. She went out. For the first time since the illness, she felt the sun on her face, but even its promise of warmth did not make her smile.

CHAPTER ELEVEN

Hunger

EATH, THE VISITOR, had stayed long that year and taken many Anishinabeg to the next world. Those left behind had the task of going on with life even as the harshest snow fell, the bitter cold deepened, the game hid, and the fish sank deeper into the lake. Now, as Omakayas began to gain a little strength, she wished heartily to eat and craved any sort of food at all. But there was only enough cornmeal in the morning for a few mouthfuls of mush, only enough wild rice for a handful each during the day. The family scrounged a potato, sometimes a bit of bannock. No meat once the fish and dried venison from the meat cache were gone.

Omakayas was strong enough to bring in wood, though she trembled as she walked. Mama improved slowly, too; at least she got stronger physically. Her face remained unchanging and sad, and her eyes remained haunted by the sorrow of Neewo's loss.

◄○►

Deydey was recovering so slowly that he didn't have the strength to hunt. Though he tried to fish, he hadn't much luck and could not stand the cold for long. He had to borrow against next year's furs. The family ran up a bill at the traders, bought expensive salt pork.

One day, he notched his counting stick and spoke to Omakayas.

"The trader will have all of next year's furs by the time winter is finished," he said, "unless some game throws itself at us! Or unless I can get him another way."

His eyes flashed and the shadow of a grin twisted on his face, the intrigue of the old Deydey who'd never been sick.

"Bring me the chess game," he said to Omakayas.

She knew just where it was, that precious set that had belonged to Deydey's grandfather, the man who had taught him this chimookoman game. The chess set was always reverently kept in its own blanket, hidden in a corner of the room with the medicine bags and Deydey's ceremonial clothes. Wrapped in red cloth, it was considered something very special. Every few days, Deydey took it out to play solitary games and try to teach the strategies to others. Carefully, now, she bore it in her arms to Deydey.

He took the chess set, and there before the fire he arranged the pieces in their special order. The pieces were hand-carved of maple, finely grained. The queen, or ogema, wore a small pointed hat. Omakayas liked the horse, its neck curved and strong. The pawns were little round-headed people. The bishop looked just like Father Baraga, the priest who walked miles in his snowshoes to baptize, stealing souls from the other mission and also from the manitous. The little towers at the ends, those that moved so honestly and directly, were Omakayas's favorite pieces.

The two began to play. Deydey usually beat her in short time, but today she managed through desperate measures to think ahead far enough to draw the game out to a phenomenal length.

"Geget chi wohningeyz," said Deydey, approvingly. "Good job! My girl, maybe you should be the one to play the trader."

Deydey's compliments were so rare that when he

gave them Omakayas at first didn't absorb what she'd heard. It took until later, lying curled in her blanket, for the warmth that his approval gave her to sink into place around her heart, warming her as she fell into a good sleep.

The next day, Deydey took the chess board and headed to the trader's to play for supplies. He did not allow his family to come and watch him, for those who gathered were often rough: layarounds, drinkers, wintering voyageurs who idled their time with gambling and trader's rum. Fishtail and LaPautre were there, however, and it was from LaPautre's daughter Twilight that the girls heard the details of the game.

As Twilight told it, Deydey had walked in humbly, played poorly at first, causing the trader to raise the stakes. Then Deydey dragged the game out awkwardly until the trader thought he was unbeatable. He was sure that he was going to win, and felt confident enough to agree, laughingly, to cancel part of Deydey's debt. That was when Deydey pounced! In six swift moves Deydey finished him off. Deydey's triumph resulted in a small square of salt pork, a bit of flour, some dried apples, and a bladder of fish oil. That last item, none of the children were happy to see.

Dosed every morning with the awful stuff, they

were sure to stay healthy now. But the price was high. Drinking the oil down gagged Omakayas. Tears came to her eyes and more than once she wished her father was not quite so good at the game of chess.

<o>

Old Tallow was sitting by the fire, cleaning and oiling each part of her ancient, frail gun. She usually had more luck with her sharp lance, but claimed that out of hunger her arms were weakening and her aim with the razor-keen instrument was off. Even her snares, set so cleverly just where a rabbit usually wanted to and needed to hop, yielded almost none at all. Rabbits were suddenly dying from a rabbit disease that seemed to eat up their insides.

"Neshkey!" Old Tallow split a poor waboose, rabbit, and opened its skinny body to show that the creature was mush inside, a bloody pudding as the result of disease.

"Probably a sickness brought by the chimookoman, too!" she growled. Since the death of Neewo, she refused to attempt to speak to anyone who was not Anishinabe. The traders got her cold eye, the missionaries her hard glare, the few other white visitors who chanced onto the island received from Old Tallow no welcome. She blamed them for the disease. She blamed them for the poor quality of game and the scarcity of food—naturally, when so many animals were hunted for sale to white traders for fur, there would be fewer left to eat for survival. The only thing wrong with their lives that she could not blame on the chimookoman was the weather, though she tried.

"Their loud voices scare off the sun! The sun is afraid of their hairy faces!"

"If the sun is not afraid of your face," said Deydey, "I'm sure no chimookoman could make it hide."

"You are mixed blood," jeered Old Tallow, pleased to be in a mock exchange of insults, "wisikodewinini, half-burnt wood. Am I speaking to the white half or the Anishinabe?"

"Go ahead, cut my arm," offered Deydey, "see if you can divide the white blood from the red blood."

"Saaa." Old Tallow looked toward Nokomis for help, but she just raised her eyebrows. "Mikwam! If you're so strong, melt away this ice."

"You're the hotheaded one," said Deydey. "You melt it."

Nobody could, for after a few weeks of kind weather the earth had frozen with a vengeance, and spring seemed far away. Omakayas was tired of all the different kinds of ice around her. There was the just plain ice, the kind you couldn't see through, that covered the lake and hid the water and the fish below. That was the ice she had to help Nokomis chop every day from the deep hole they fished through. The fish were biting only rarely. They could fish all day and not even come up with a skinny lake trout. The nets they lowered through the ice hole came up frozen solid the moment they reached the surface, of course. Empty ice nets! There was the ice on the oiled paper window, ice on the inside of the cabin walls on cold mornings, ice on the frozen paths and ice in the water bucket. Transparent ice, white ice, ice so black and solid you couldn't see through it.

"If only we could eat ice. If only ice was food!" said Pinch. As he said this, into his mind's eye came the picture of the berries he'd stuffed into his mouth last summer. Mama was right. If only he had them now!

All Omakayas was interested in, she thought one evening as she fell asleep, was thin ice. Then no ice. Melting ice. She thought that until she had her dream.

Nokomis put charcoal on her face one night, sent her to bed with no food, told her to remember her dreams, if she should have any. Omakayas knew that Nokomis wanted her to search for and find a spirit helper, someone great in the spirit world who would help her to recover her will to live. Omakayas tried to make herself better, to stop dwelling on worthless sadnesses. Omakayas couldn't help it. She didn't care about the world. Still, she did as she was told and went to sleep determined to remember any dream she might have.

No dream. As before, in the dead of winter, her dreams were blank. The moon shifted one quarter, then Nokomis tried again. Nothing. At last, when Omakayas had a particularly slow day, Nokomis made sure that she tried to dream yet again. She smoothed the dry powdery black charcoal onto Omakayas' face and sang to her as she fell asleep.

That night, Omakayas dreamed.

Everything was ice in her dream, and she was sliding on it. Faster, slipperier, she was sliding through the woods and then down to the lakeshore. Something drew her onto the icy lake shore and although she knew the ice covered the rocks she kept walking, exploring. Before her, there was a cave. She entered.

"Ahneen," said a soft voice from deep in the darkness.

"Ahneen," said Omakayas, "where are you?"

In a glimmer of light, a motherly woman showed herself. She was dressed in the most beautiful furs and her face was very kind, her eyes deep, thrilling, wild.

Black fur rippled against her dark skin. She opened her mouth. Her teeth were long and sharp, but there was nothing to fear.

"I'm going to help you," said the woman. "I feel sorry for you, and I love you. Just remember to give me tobacco. I'm the bear spirit woman. I knew your great-grandma and great-grandpa. They live with me now."

Omakayas woke slowly. It was like floating to the surface of a warm depth of feeling. She wanted to stay in the dream, but in just the same way that she always bobbed to the water's surface in the summer, no matter how hard she tried to sit on the lake bottom, she lost her struggle and knew after a time that she was fully awake. The dream was gone.

Later that day, Omakayas told Nokomis about the dream.

Immediately, Nokomis took her aside and brought her to the corner of the house near the window of oiled paper. There, sitting across from her, Nokomis smoothed Omakayas's hair to each side with her worn hands and smiled lovingly into her granddaughter's eyes.

"These bear people want to help you. You must not forget to give your helper tobacco whenever you think of her. She's with you, your lady. She's going to help you. She will be looking out for you in this world."

◄◦►

The only thing good about this time of winter was the stories. While the snow and ice still held fast, Nokomis told them tales about the world of manitous and windigos, tales of Nanabozho, the comical teacher. Those last were favorites of the girls. Maybe because she so often felt small and helpless, Omakayas thought long about one particular tale Nokomis told. She loved to hear it when the flames jumped and the frozen world outside the small cabin was dark. One night she asked her grandmother to tell it once again.

"Nokomis, very soon, the ice will break and the lake will start moving. The animals will stir and the frogs will wake up! I know there will be no more stories until next winter. So please, the diving muskrat one now?"

Nokomis nodded, pleased that Omakayas asked, for this story was an important teaching story, or adisokaan. While her fingers swiftly flew at her quillwork, she told the story of how the earth began.

NANABOZHO AND MUSKRAT MAKE AN EARTH

—◄○►—

Maywizah, Maywizah, long time ago. Rain started. More rain, as though it would never quit. The water rose so fast that our Nanabozho ran to the top of a hill. The water followed him. At the top of the hill there was a pine tree. Nanabozho climbed the tree. Still the water kept rising. He said to the tree, "Brother, stretch yourself." The tree stretched twice as long. He climbed some more, then asked the tree to stretch again. The tree stretched four times. That's how tall it was.

Finally, the tree told Nanabozho that he couldn't do any more for him. That was as high as the tree could go. But then the water stopped. Nanabozho was standing at the top of the tree. He had his head back and the water was up to his mouth.

After a while, Nanabozho noticed that there were animals playing in the water, Beaver, Muskrat, and Otter. Nanabozho spoke first to Otter, asking, "Brother, could you go down and get some earth? If you do that, I will make an earth for you and me to live on."

Otter said to Nanabozho, "I will try."

Away he went, down to the bottom of the water. But Otter didn't get halfway to the bottom. He drowned, then floated up to the top. Nanabozho caught hold of the otter and looked into the otter's paws and mouth, but didn't find any dirt. Then Nanabozho blew on Otter and brought him back to life.

"Did you see anything?" he asked.

"No," said Otter.

The next animal Nanabozho spoke to was Beaver. He asked him to go after some earth down below and said, "If you do, I'll make an earth for us to live on."

Beaver said, "I'll try," and went down. Beaver was gone a long time. Pretty soon he floated to the top of the water. He had also drowned. Nanabozho caught hold of the beaver and blew on him. When Beaver came to, Nanabozho examined his paws and mouth to see if there was any dirt, but he couldn't find anything.

"Did you see any earth at the bottom?" Nanabozho asked Beaver.

"Yes, I did," said the beaver. "I saw it, but I couldn't get any of it."

These animals had tried and failed.

Muskrat was also playing around in the water. Nanabozho didn't think much about the muskrat, because he was so small, just a little animal, too weak. But after a while he said to him, "Why don't you try and go after some of that dirt, too?"

Muskrat said, "I'll try," and he dived down.

Nanabozho waited and waited a long time for Muskrat to come up to the top of the water. When he floated up to the top, he was dead from his exertion. Nanabozho caught hold of Muskrat and looked him over. Muskrat had his paws closed up tight. His mouth was shut, too. Nanabozho opened Muskrat's front paw and found a grain of earth in it. He took it. In his other front paw Nanabozho found another little grain, and one grain of dirt in each of his hind paws. There was another grain in his mouth.

When he'd found these five grains, Nanabozho blew on Muskrat until he came back to life. Then Nanabozho took the grains of earth in the palm of his hand. He held them up to the sun to dry them out. When they were all dry, he threw them around onto the water. A little island rose. The four went onto the island—Nanabozho, Otter, Beaver, and Muskrat. Nan-

abozho got more earth on the island, and threw it all around. The island got bigger. It got larger every time Nanabozho threw out another handful of dirt. The animals at the bottom of the water, whoever was there, all came up to the top of the water and went to the island, this earth we are on today.

—<o>—

Omakayas knew that her Nokomis told her this story for a larger reason than just because she asked for it. She thought many times of the muskrat diving down, down, down for that little bit of dirt that made the world. She imagined Muskrat finally pulling to the very bottom and grasping that bit of earth in its tiny paws.

"If such a small animal could do so much," Nokomis always said, after she'd finished the story, "your efforts are important, too."

As if he had understood Grandma's story, Andeg made his own effort. Her crow hunted mice these lean days with more savage intentions than when merely keeping them away from his family of humans. He hunted for survival. The bird eagerly awaited any mouse who dared enter the house. Hungrily, Andeg dropped and struck, hard, killing the little animal and quickly eating it. Andeg also hunted in the woods for seeds and nuts cached by squirrels. That winter, Andeg found a little hollow in a tree next to the cabin. Some squirrel had filled the hollow with acorns, seeds, hazelnuts. Enough to feed the family for a day or two!

"Neshkey," said Mama, her hands full one morning. "Look what that good bird found for us!"

Andeg was looking at the food cache as though he wasn't quite sure he'd meant to share, but Mama was pleased. She scattered a big load of acorns on the hearth stones and looked at them with satisfaction before she began to break the little shells with her smoothest pounding rock. She shelled the acorns, ground them fine, roasted them with a bit of cornmeal, and that night the family had sweet acorn cakes. From the last cone of maple sugar, she made a taste of syrup for them all, and that night, at least, they went to sleep with a comfortable warmth in their stomachs. All of them, before sleeping, thanked Andeg, who, though he usually slept outside, was invited in that night. He sat above the fire on a thick twig perch Deydey had fastened between the mortared stones. Andeg preened his feathers, very glad to be so warm, bobbed his sleek head, and blinked his brilliant eyes.

Tomorrow, resolved Omakayas now that she had a bit of strength, she would make her small, important effort like the muskrat. She would go out with Andeg and find more squirrel caches in the woods. She didn't reckon on her own weakness, however, nor could she ever have imagined the swiftness of Old Tallow's justice.

—◄o►—

The day dawned pure and cold. Nokomis and Mama mixed up some water with the thin paste of acorn flour left from the night before. Deydey came in with a fish so tiny and poor-looking that, in spite of their hunger, everyone laughed out loud when he lifted it proudly into the air. Everyone, that is, except Mama. She just rested her eyes a little more softly on her husband than usual, and went on with her beadwork. Omakayas, ready to do her part, dressed in her warmest clothes, wrapped lengths of rabbit-skin around her feet, put makazins over them and then, Andeg on her shoulder, went to look for the squirrel caches.

Although she had fished with Nokomis, this was the first time Omakayas had ventured into the woods since the day she had entered the cabin. On that day, she had followed the sickness inside and determined to do battle with the evil spirit of the disease. She had lost her beloved Neewo. Now she decided that she would not lose any of her family to the weakness of hunger. She would find food. Somewhere. Dizziness overcame her. Her knees felt watery and her blood ran thin. She paused, holding onto a tree, and made her way toward the woods beyond. First, she had to pass Old Tallow's place, and she narrowed her eyes at the path and stepped forward with determined quickness, prepared not to stop until Andeg told her where to find more nuts and acorns. She didn't reckon on the yellow dog.

He was there in her path as she neared Old Tallow's cabin. She wouldn't look at him, she decided, but she couldn't help remembering the words his look had given her last summer. *Wait until next time! I'll get you then! I'll get you when no one is around.* What could he do to her? Even in her weakness, she would be mentally stronger, she would show him no fear. But as though he sensed the truth of her condition, and not the determined pluck of her heart, the yellow dog stepped forward. As always, he snarled and then retreated when Omakayas grabbed a stick. When she brandished the stick, however, a spinning haze of brilliant dots flooded up before her eyes. Suddenly it was as though she stepped over the edge of a black cliff. She stumbled, fainted to the ground. The yellow dog lunged forward. Andeg screamed and tore with his beak at the dog's eyes, but the dog was eager, at last, to get the better of a human. As the clumsiest hunting dog of Old Tallow's pack, he needed to stand tall over something, even if only a sick little girl.

Omakayas groped for her stick, but suddenly the yellow dog had it in his teeth. He growled, worried the stick as though he'd caught a gopher, then dropped it and with an eager bite tore into the blanket that fell from her arm. With a vicious lunge, he bit Omakayas above the wrist and jumped back, eyes blazing with cowardly triumph. Omakayas tried to yell, but her voice stuck in her throat, a squeak. She felt a rushing blackness overwhelm her again, tried to throw herself upward, tried to growl back and challenge the dog. With excitement, though, the dog realized he had her at his mercy at last. He jumped forward again. This time, he fell upon her leg and bit deep. Omakayas heard a loud scream, her own scream, and pain blotted her sight then as she swirled into the dark.

She woke a moment later, in Old Tallow's arms.

"What happened?"

Nearby, the yellow dog cringed and tried to slink away from Old Tallow's glare. Seeing that Omakayas was all right, Old Tallow carefully put the girl down. With a swift, bearlike swipe, she grabbed the dog and held him by the scruff of the neck with one hand. He whimpered, and snarled at Omakayas as though to say, *She made me do it!* Old Tallow shook her head, sadly, and lifted her ax. Ignoring Omakayas, who panted weakly on the snowy ground, Old Tallow spoke to her dog as she would to a human. Sadly and firmly, holding him by the neck, she told the dog what he had done.

"Didn't I warn you, didn't I say to you, didn't I tell you many times that you must never hurt this one? Yes, n'dai, you look at me now with pleading eyes, but I spared you many times before. Each time I spared your life, I always told you what would happen if you were so foolish again. Now, my foolish friend, you must die."

With that, Old Tallow brought the blunt end of her ax down on the yellow dog's head. He crumpled to the ground.

"Ai! My auntie!"

The yellow dog had hated her, perhaps even meant to kill her, but Omakayas hadn't counted on such a cruel and sudden end to the dog's cowardly life. Old Tallow's justice was harsh. Her sentence was carried out in an instant, but that didn't mean that her heart was hard or that she didn't mourn for her friend. It just meant that Omakayas was more important. The last that Omakayas saw of the yellow dog, he was bundled in Old Tallow's arms. The strong old woman was walking away, and in her step there was the sadness of parting with an old but dangerously foolish friend.

Omakayas got slowly to her feet, wobbled forward, and knew that she would have to return to the cabin. She still wasn't strong enough to hunt for food. With Andeg's encouragement, she made it back to the door and fell through, her vision darkening. Her stomach creaked, so empty it stuck to the back of her body. She needed Grandma's help to dress the bites that throbbed and stung. They must have food, they must have food. Soon they must eat, she knew, or they would all lie in the ground with the two who had gone before.

◄O►

It was the great buck One Horn who saved them, who

gave them his life. Grandma woke two mornings later and called Deydey to her side to talk, for she was so weak from hunger she could only sit wrapped in her blanket by the fire.

"I dreamed last night," she told him. "And now you must do everything just as I say."

Deydey listened intently.

"Take the small path to the north, that leads past the fish camp," said Grandma, gesturing slowly. She squinted. Looked deeper into her dream. Nodded slowly. "When you come to the tallest of the trees, go toward the lake, then around the rocks and back into the trees. There, the buck will wait for you."

Deydey knew when Grandma dreamed, especially in this extremity, it was a true dream and must be followed. First, however, he prepared himself carefully to meet the animal's spirit. He washed, put on his best clothing, new makazins, and had Mama comb and braid his hair. He cleaned and oiled his new gun and prepared it with extra care. Then he went immediately out and followed Grandma's directions exactly. Just as she had said, in the clearing past the rocks and back in the trees, One Horn was waiting. The great buck stood still in the calm light. Deydey lifted his gun, breathed his hopes. Then thanks. One shot. The shot went true. One Horn died easily, right then.

Deydey gave tobacco to the deer's spirit and thanked him, brought back as much as he could carry, then buried the rest of the deer in snow. Returning, he gave the venison to his starving family and to Tallow, who shared it out to Auntie Muskrat, to LaPautre's hungry children, and to Fishtail.

That night, as Omakayas ate the stew of venison that Mama cooked, she felt herself grow stronger with each bite. She remembered the day she and Angeline stood before the beauty of One Horn. They had looked on him, amazed, and he did not run away. Had he known, at that time, that they would need his very existence? Again, Omakayas remembered the proud,

soft radiance of his brown eyes. She closed her eyes and saw One Horn feasted, honored, and decorated with her grandmother's finest beadwork. Opening her eyes again, she thanked the animal for saving her life, and then, just as she finished thinking this solemn thought, Pinch, whose belly was full, backed up too close to the hearth and set the seat of his pants on fire.

"Mama!" He jumped away, a little flame shooting from his rear. In sudden inspiration, he sat down directly in the water bucket. Everybody looked at him, at first in shock, and then once he was seen to have suffered no harm it was Mama, first of all, who started to laugh. And Pinch laughed, too. Laughed so hard that he wedged his behind farther into the bucket, and could not get out. Laughed and laughed. Harder and harder! Ever after that terrible winter, as though he understood from then on how important it was to be funny, Pinch gave laughter to them all. He became a joker, a trick player, and joked on himself as well as others. Perhaps it was that first saving laugh, the best thing any of them had heard since before the death of Neewo, that made him proud. He had saved his family, in a way, every bit as much as One Horn.

The great deer had saved their bodies, and Pinch's absurd jump had saved their souls, for Nokomis said shortly after that her own grandmother had believed that the soul of the Anishinabeg is made of laughter. If there is no laughter, the soul dies. Pinch brought laughter back to life. He brought their souls back into their bodies. The harder they laughed the more they knew, now, they would survive.

Zeegwun

(SPRING)

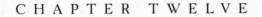

CHAPTER TWELVE

Maple Sugar Time

VERYONE IN THE CABIN heard it—the far-off creaking and groaning, the boom of the lake ice. The lake had started to move again. The ice was breaking up. Once the waves began, huge sheets of ice shoved against each other, pushing towers into the air. Nokomis, Mama, Deydey, Pinch, Angeline, and Omakayas all ran outside, gazed on the horizon, and saw the crackling and snapping waves of the ice. They felt the surge of lake water in their blood. They knew, at last, that the back of winter was entirely broken.

Omakayas grinned. Her smile was now whole— new teeth had grown in over the winter. She was older. Soon, spring plants would poke up through dead leaves.

The curled heads of ferns. Buds, roots, fresh new leaves. Fat lake trout would sleepily rise from the bottom, hungry to be caught. Siskowet and whitefish would fill their nets. They would be able to think of something other than the next bite of food. They would live again, truly live.

◄◦►

Angeline went to the mission school every day now. She was learning to write her name in Zhaganashimowin, the white man's language, and she taught Omakayas the things she learned. Using a pointed stick to write in wet mud, Angeline showed Omakayas and Nokomis the meaningful signs, which looked like odd tracks.

"What animal would leave these?" Omakayas teased.

"Be patient," Nokomis counseled. "Let's find out what your sister has learned."

"They're letters," Angeline said, eager to share her knowledge. "One follows the next. You look at them, just like tracks. You read them. They have a meaning and a sound."

"Howah! That's a good idea! Like our picture writing," Nokomis said.

The girls knew people like Fishtail's father, Day

Thunder, who kept the records for the religious gatherings, the Midewiwin, and etched stories and songs on scrolls made of birchbark. They had seen some birchbark writing, and they knew that Nokomis could etch pictures into bark, too. She also knew where certain marks had been placed upon lake rocks long ago. Some of the marks were made by the spirits, some were made by humans; others were drawn by a giant race of people who had lived on earth in the old days and had disappeared. Angeline's description of the white man's tracks interested Omakayas, in spite of herself.

The system sounded incredible—sounds, meanings—but the idea made sense. Thereafter, to learn the Zhaganashimowin letters and sounds became a source of amusement, for the evenings were still long.

"Aaaaay," said Angeline, tracing the letter on the rough stone of the hearth.

"Aaaaay," said Omakayas. "Beee. Seee. Deee." She learned to make the pictures, and she learned to make the sounds, slowly, all of them. Words would follow, Angeline said, but Omakayas could not believe that would happen. She remembered that last winter, before the sickness began, she had seen Fishtail walking from the mission school. Had he learned to make the white man's tracks? Had he learned to write his name? Had he learned to read the words of the treaties so that his people could not be cheated of land?

"Boozhoo, nindinaweymaganidok," called Fishtail one day.

He was at the door of the cabin, calling hello to his relatives. Grandma greeted him kindly, for he was ashamed of his thinness and weakness. She brought him inside. His hair was short and wild as porcupine quills, his face starved and sallow with grief. No longer did he wear the proud, somewhat disdainful look he'd worn

when walking seriously along through the woods, his pipe cradled in his arms. He was still hawk-keen, with a strong and handsome face, but his eyes were more human, humble, gentle. He gazed pityingly down at Omakayas and touched her hair.

"Little Frog," he said, and there was a hint of smile in his voice, as though to see her brought him comfort, "my good wife loved you as her little sister. You made her laugh with your quick ways. She told me you were much loved by the bear people. She told me, also, that you had a bird named Andeg."

"Andeg!" called Omakayas, and like a dark arrow her crow swooped down and landed on her shoulder. Andeg looked curiously at Fishtail, wondering whether he possibly had something to feed him. The bird danced from foot to foot, took a strand of Omakayas's hair in his beak but did not pull. Andeg tucked the hair behind Omakayas's ear just like a grandfather soothing a child to sleep!

"Owah," said Fishtail, in wonder, "you *are* much beloved by the creatures."

Over his shoulder Fishtail carried a blanket, meaning that he had much to say and planned to spend the night. Deydey greeted him, holding him by the arms, and Nokomis stirred up the fire, adding a stick there, a bit of wood in exactly the right spot to make it blaze up cheerfully. Mama had made a good stew, filled with flaky chunks of fish, and the kettle bubbled hot, hung above the hearth fire.

Fishtail took off his big moose-hide mitts and Angeline dished up a wooden bowl of the soup, eager for him to sit and warm himself. Because he was related as a cross-cousin, and also because he had been the husband of her friend, she was familiar around him and not shy at all. She tried to cheer him up, to bring a smile to his face by teasing him gently.

"Deydey needs snowshoes all winter, but you," Angeline pointed with her lips at Fishtail, "already have yours on, eh?"

Fishtail gave a little smile, but there was still too much sadness in him to laugh. He waggled his feet—they were big, it was true, almost as big as snowshoes, as big as Old Tallow's huge long ones.

"Ayah! They come in handy!" Fishtail acknowledged. "If I lose a paddle I've always got one attached."

He took great gulps of the fish broth, and slowly, feeling better, he warmed to the talk with Deydey. They were planning this year's sugaring, a time everyone looked forward to with joy and excitement, as much as ricing, maybe even more. For when the maple sap began to run it meant that warmer days, pleasant sun, all the beauties of spring were close at hand.

"This sweetness just at the raggedy end of winter!" Nokomis was excited as a girl, and her enthusiasm made everyone smile with affection. "But the creator expects us to be ready. While you talk, you men work!"

She herself was smoothing out a paddle to use in stirring the syrup, and just the day before Deydey had started hollowing a peeled, smooth piece of basswood for a trough. Now Deydey asked for the use of Omakayas's gun-barrel flesher. She brought it quickly from its place in the corner. She was glad to find another use for Deydey's gift besides the usual unpleasant one of scraping hides. Taking the hide flesher in his hands, Deydey sharpened the end well on his sharpening stone. Holding the barrel in his strong fingers like a chisel, he hit the other end with his mallet, tapping long slices of wood away from the inside of the log. Every strip of wood he tapped from the inside, Pinch grabbed and threw into the fire. The trough grew smoother, deeper. Fishtail, meanwhile, smoked peacefully and looked into the leaping flames.

"You get to work, too!" Angeline said, smiling. She tossed him a bit of venison jerky, though, for him to chew on when he finished smoking his kinnikinnick.

◂o▸

The family sugaring place was at the other end of the island. When they traveled to the sugar bush, the family packed as lightly as possible. Once they arrived, they would use the frames set up last year for their big sugaring house. There was a smaller wigwam where the tools were stored. There usually was a food cache buried last fall, filled with good things that had lain far beneath the snow. But this year, Deydey had already made a trip to the end of the island and raided the cache. To keep from starving, they had already eaten their store during the lean moon.

When they arrived, the first thing Mama did was unroll the reed mats for the roof of the shelter, then the blankets, then take out new paddles and the cooking pot. Deydey dragged a big kettle and more wooden troughs and paddles from the small storage house. Anything that wasn't at the sugaring place, or anything that broke or wore out, they could make for themselves. Nokomis and Omakayas arranged the food they'd brought. There were packets of split, dried fish, a makuk of special powdered fish, moose meat, a little manomin traded for with deer meat, smoked fish, and a bag of dried pumpkin flowers to thicken soups.

"Neshkey," said Nokomis, happy they had so much. "We'll have a good feast."

Once a soup was in the making, Nokomis left Angeline to stir and called Omakayas to come along and help chop taps to open the maples.

The two wandered a bit until Nokomis found a good ironwood tree. She took out her sharp hatchet and expertly chopped into the tree at regular angles. She made a series of perfect cuts down the side of the tree, and then chopped sideways and split from the tree ten perfect wedges of the hard ironwood. She did this until she had a huge sackful of wedges, which Omakayas lugged back to the camp.

For two days they prepared, knowing that the sap was just about to start running. There was a feeling to that time before the sap began, a quietness that had the going-out taste of winter. All that happened in the snow and cold, the storytelling and the sadness, too, was left behind. Omakayas opened herself to the warming wind. Before them, the sweetness of the maple waited, the warmth of the sun.

—◦—

Omakayas, Twilight, and Little Bee carted heavy rocks from the lakeshore to weigh down the makuks, and then hauled wood for the fire. Omakayas's arms were tired, and her cousins', too. They complained impatiently to each other as they hunted for the right-sized stones or hauled load after load of wood in their arms, dumping it near the big kettle, which was boiling and steaming away. As yet, not one taste of the maple syrup! Just the cold, sweet sap. It was always this way before the first taste. The boiling down seemed to take so endlessly long! Pinch watched jealously. Jumped on a log to observe Grandma's paddle when it came up and dipped back down again. Still not ready. Still not. Still not.

Then ready.

Onto the surface of a big makuk filled with clean snow, Grandma dribbled a thin dark-gold stream of syrup. Pinch could hardly wait for it to cool—gum sugar! He grabbed while it was still a soft rope, swung the strand into his mouth, and ran, for once quiet instead of yelling, only because his mouth was stuffed. Andeg was caught up in the excitement and he jumped from foot to foot, nearly tumbling from Omakayas's shoulder as Angeline poured out more syrup and then helped Grandma ladle the rest into a sugaring trough. He pecked at a bit of the syrup, but didn't seem to like the sticky feel of it on his beak, and shook his head comically. He put his head in the snow, wiped his beak back and forth, but couldn't remove the hardening syrup. He flew up to a low branch and glared down at them, betrayed, preening his feathers, making his feathers sticky with the syrup too.

"Minopogwud," said Omakayas, licking up a dollop of thick syrup.

The first taste usually made her smile. Not this time. Sadness overwhelmed her when she tasted the sweetness. She instantly recalled the special day she spent with Neewo on the shore of the lake. On that day, long ago last summer, she had freed him from the tight bonds of his tikinagun, let him tumble and play. When it came time for her to put him back, she'd sweetened his confinement by placing her last bit of sugar on his tongue.

"Chickadee, my brother," she cried to Neewo under her breath.

She looked around. Pinch was running and jumping, striking out with a stick and pretending to hunt doves. Nokomis was stirring the syrup using a dancing kind of smooth movement with her arms. Mama was putting together a stew and Deydey was off somewhere with Fishtail, planning ceremonies that would be held during the sugaring, not far from their camp. Angeline looked at her and said, "Neshemay, go get some more wood!"

She, Omakayas, was the only one thinking of Neewo. The knowledge made her lonely. If only she could talk to him, look into his cheerful, upslanted eyes, share with him her feelings that he never laughed at, play with him in her arms. She missed him terribly, so much so that her heart seemed to drop right through her stomach with a thud. Muffling her cries, she ran from camp straight out into the woods.

Angeline was surprised. Usually her sister did not fetch wood with such enthusiasm.

"Howah!" she called after her little sister. "Megwetch!"

Omakayas knew that she would not come back, however, and Angeline could fetch her own wood. She ran with an angry heart. Breathing hard, skimming away as fast as she could, she got away from everyone before she sat down on a little patch of dry, sunny ground. At last, it was all right to sob and sob, to let herself cry as much as she wanted to. But the strange thing was, as soon as she sat down she didn't feel like crying anymore. She heard the song of the white throated sparrow, and was soothed by the piercing refrain. She smiled. Neewo's spirit was comforting her. Her eyelids got heavy, the sun warmed her, and she was just about lost in a dream when she was startled by the crackle of sticks and twigs, the shuffle of feet, the interested snuffling, and most of all the commanding and unmistakeable odor of bear.

They were with her.

Standing quiet at the edge of the little spot of sun, the two young bears gazed curiously, knowingly, at Omakayas. Andeg flew down suddenly, as though he, the little crow, had to protect her from her brothers! The two bears startled a bit at the crow's angry charge, but then shrugged and ignored him.

"It's okay," said Omakayas, and Andeg returned to her shoulder.

The bears continued to look closely at Omakayas, peering with their dim bear eyes, taking in every dot of her scent, remembering it all, knowing. Omakayas wished that she had something to give them—she had run away from camp with nothing more than a handful of spirit tobacco in her pocket. They kept looking at her, waiting and watching. The only thing she could think of to give them, in the end, was some human advice. She decided to warn them about other humans and the dangers they posed.

"There's a woman," Omakayas said, softly, "her name is Old Tallow. She's my aunt, but *you* must stay away from her."

The young bears' ears twitched a little. They seemed to listen closely. "Be careful, too," Omakayas went on, "when you see something better to eat than usual, out in the woods. If it's hanging up out of reach, there might be a pit underneath. That's a trap. You'll fall in and die. And guns. My brothers, run fast from men carrying big sticks on their shoulders. Stay away from them. Don't go near the humans, either the Anishinabeg or the chimookomanug. Stay deep in the woods. Hide if you hear Old Tallow's dogs."

Omakayas reached into her pocket and took out the little handful of tobacco. She put the tobacco on the ground. When she did, she knew she was asking for something, but she wasn't sure what it was. Words she had not expected came from her lips.

"Will you give me your medicine?"

She asked this, but her voice was uncertain. She really didn't know what she meant. She felt embarrassed at herself. "I'm pitiful," she said, just as her grandmother did sometimes when praying. "I don't know anything. I want to know your medicine. I want to be like Nokomis. I want strong medicines to save my family."

Tears came into Omakayas's eyes and she could hardly see, hardly noticed when the bears wheeled and silently disappeared. "Help me," she whispered to the ground, "help me."

Once she'd finished talking, she lifted her face and looked around. Her bear brothers had vanished, and she felt better. She set to work gathering a huge load of dry sticks, dead branches torn off during the winter by heavy snow and ice. As she was piling the branches higher and higher, she saw, on the side of a dry piece of birch wood, the gray hoof of a mushroom. A tiny voice whispered in her head, a low voice, muttering. When she picked up the branch, the voice grew louder but she still couldn't make out individual words. She added the branch to her pile, bound the pile with a thong, carried it back to the camp on her shoulders.

From time to time, as she walked back to camp through the woods, she heard a small sound, a word or two, muffled under the snow and leaves. By the time she reached the sugaring camp she felt a little bit afraid. What were these voices? What did the whispering mean? Standing in the clearing, safe, she peered into the maze of branches and undergrowth. Shining scraps of snow lighted the ground as far as she could see. The sounds of voices, small and whispery, still floated from the depth of the woods.

"What took you so long?" Angeline said, a bit annoyed. She'd burned her finger in the process of pouring some hot syrup, and she was hurting badly. "What's wrong with you?"

Omakayas put down her load and told her sister that she had something important to do.

"So do I!" Angeline yelled back. Omakayas walked over to Nokomis. She was fashioning small cones of birchbark for the sugar. She had saved a string of duck bills, too, that she'd fill with hard sugar for a special treat. Omakayas sat down beside her.

"Nokomis," said Omakayas, her voice soft and troubled, "I talked to my bear brothers. I listened to them like you told me."

Immediately, Nokomis set down her work, wiped her hands on her skirt, and brought her granddaughter over to a wide fallen log to sit with her. She smoothed Omakayas's hair down to either side, and looked keenly into her eyes and face.

"Wait." Intent and serious, Nokomis filled her red stone pipe with tobacco. It was a sign that she was going to hear something important, and she took a long time perfectly tamping her pipe, which was good, because during that time Omakayas had the chance to think about just what she would tell her grandmother. When Nokomis lit the pipe and drew on it, the coals burning, the sweetness of the smoke filled the air around them and made a small, holy room in which they sat, their minds close together.

"I talked to them," Omakayas repeated.

"What did you say?"

"I told them how to be careful of humans."

"That's good," said Nokomis, reflecting, "unless we need meat. What did you say next?"

"I asked my bear brothers for help," said Omakayas carefully.

"What did they do?"

"I don't know."

"What do you mean?" A wreath of smoke swirled around Nokomis's face.

"I asked them for medicine," said Omakayas, "and when I looked up, they were gone. But as I walked back here, I heard voices." Omakayas looked quickly at her grandmother to see if she understood, and as she only nodded, Omakayas went on talking. "They were odd voices, all different types of voices."

"Did they come from the woods?"

"Yes."

"Did you understand what they were saying to you?"

"No."

"Neither did I," said Nokomis, her voice pleased, "not at first."

Omakayas looked at her grandmother, remembering the time she had asked whether the plant medicines had ever spoken to her. Nokomis took the pipe from her lips and gave Omakayas a long and searching look of regard. Her eyes beamed out a quiet message of love. Nokomis understood the meaning of what had happened, understood why the voices had spoken, understood what it meant for Omakayas's future, and was proud and glad to have a granddaughter who was chosen to be a healer.

"Even now, today, I sometimes don't know what they are saying. But then, I'm old and getting weak," said Nokomis. "You are young and strong, Omakayas, and as I teach you about my medicines you'll hear them more clearly."

"Do they talk to you every day?"

"Oh, no, but often enough."

"Why were they talking all at once?" Omakayas wondered.

Nokomis thought for a while. "I think they talk to each other all the time," she said, "but our minds are not always peaceful enough to hear them."

◄○►

Nokomis told Omakayas that bears dig for medicine. They are a different kind of people from us. They don't use fire, but they laugh. They hold their children. They eat the same things we do and treat themselves with medicine from certain plants. They are known as healers. Those in the bear clan are often good at healing others. Nokomis said all of these things while stirring syrup, sugaring, constantly checking and rechecking the fires, making extra makuks and cones of birchbark to hold the sugar they would have that year.

It turned out to be a good year. The sap went down into the roots during the cold nights, came up strong when the sun warmed the trunks during the day. The winter had started out bare, frosted the trees deeply, and then the deep snows had fallen. That was known as the best kind of year for maple sap. No thunderstorms marred the flavor of the sugar. No prayers for good weather went unanswered.

—<o>—

Omakayas's family sugared close to Auntie Muskrat's, and her cousins flooded into their camp, a wave of flying limbs and eager faces, ready for the vast games the children played all though the trees and brush. Omakayas forgot the bears, forgot the whispering of the plants, became a cousin within a pack of cousins, roaming the camps, stealing bits of sugar, laughing at each other. The girl cousins and her friends Two Strike, Twilight, and Little Bee played together in such a lively way. They were a tangle of girl! She even went to sleep each night with a tiny sense of anticipation in her heart. Still, she thought of Neewo. Even her cousins could not take away that sadness. The work came first, but then lengthening light in the afternoons kept the children at play outside and kept the aunts talking, the men gossiping, the grandmas reminiscing about their own playing days as small children when they roamed the sugar camps.

Always, in the near distance, sacred drums were sounding. The sound of the drums called people to the good life, a way of kindness, love, and deep respect for all

that lived. Deydey sometimes sang to help Fishtail. Often, there was a healing ceremony, a doctoring to cure the winter's illnesses. The old people talked to the young people, teaching them about the way to live as an Anishinabe in this world. Nokomis taught, but someone had to tend the sugarhouse fires, so many days she stayed instead of going to the ceremonies. Mama came and went, Angeline, too, and sometimes they brought Omakayas to the big lodge with the endlessly burning sacred fire.

Always, on entering, Omakayas walked around the fire the same way the sun travels and then she sat down in the calm of the lodge and listened to the crackle of the scented flames, waited for the throb of the drum. Pinch came, too, but he never sat still, not for an instant. He dived in and out of the lodge, snagged food wherever he could get it, fell asleep on the blankets Deydey kept spread in the corner near Fishtail and Day Thunder's drum. Pinch woke, jumped up, bolted from the lodge. He was on the move all day and night. Pinch was the quickest, the boldest, the most irritating of the boys in all of the camps.

One day, while Omakayas was busy helping Deydey, and the others were at the big lodge, Pinch made himself a small bow, strung with a bit of sewing sinew, and a couple of arrows made from sharpened plant stalks. He sneaked through the woods longing to make his big kill—if only a deer just his size would pass by, or a moose, maybe. If not that, a fish. He could surely spear a fish with one of his arrows. Pinch tramped the edge of the lake and many times edged out as far as he could go on the rocky shore. There was a small margin of water now, before the ice began, and the fish were hungry. Pinch got in plenty of shots, but none of them went true. He kept having to wade into the foot or so of freezing water to retrieve his arrows, so eventually Pinch's attention turned back to the camp. Making his way home, he resolved that he would hunt and shoot something, anything, to impress his family, especially his sisters, who thought he was a nuisance, beneath notice, as irritating as a fly.

Halfway back, Pinch nearly stumbled over the carcass of a dead deer. It had died not long ago, and lay cold and still right in his path.

"Howah!" Pinch yelled fiercely. He had an immediate thought. Drawing his arrows out of the quiver he'd constructed for himself, he managed, though with great difficulty, to stick them into the carcass of the deer. He lodged one at the heart and one at the throat. Then he gave four loud ferocious shouts. He'd made his first kill! Now there would have to be a feast for him!

"I made my first kill!" he yelled as he approached the camp.

Everyone turned to look at him. Thrilled with himself, he bounded forward in such intense excitement that he bumped straight into Deydey at the side of a kettle, just as he was pouring boiling-hot syrup into a sugaring trough!

Pinch screamed as the syrup spilled over his feet. Even through they were protected by makazins, much of the sap flooded in through the open top flap and burned poor Pinch—badly, much worse than Angeline's finger. Pinch was no silent sufferer, and yelled so loud that Omakayas thought the whole camp would came running to his side to see what was the matter. The drums were too penetrating, though, and blocked the sounds even of Pinch's pain.

Gently, Deydey removed Pinch's makazins. The burns were deep, the skin was already bubbling and dangerous looking. Pinch needed quick treatment, and most of Nokomis's medicines were back at the cabin. Deydey set out at once to fetch Nokomis, leaving Omakayas alone with Pinch, who howled miserably. Omakayas blocked out his cries in order to think, clearly, what she should do. Nokomis had left her small pouch in the sugarhouse, the one that she always carried for emergencies. That pouch contained remedies for all sorts of common problems, including burns. Omakayas remembered it, took it from its corner, and sat down near Pinch to look at his foot.

"Don't howl," she said to him, kindly and soothingly, "you'll bring all your blood to the top of your skin and make it worse."

Whether or not that was true, it seemed to scare Pinch into making some effort to control the noises he made. For the first time, he looked up at his big sister with trusting eyes.

"Help me," he whimpered, "it hurts."

That was all she needed to hear.

"I'm going to make it better," said Omakayas, and once she said this she was determined to do exactly that.

Omakayas examined him carefully. She had seen her Nokomis treat burns. Omakayas looked at and smelled the leaves and dried flowers in the birchbark packets that belonged to Nokomis. Horsemint. Omakayas removed the packet, and tried to remember what to do next. Pinch whimpered and gasped. Omakayas took out the stone Nokomis used to prepare her medicines. In the center of that stone there was a hollow, and into that natural small bowl Omakayas put the leaves that smelled summery and sharp, fresh and potent. With the other long stone Nokomis often used, Omakayas crushed them to a paste. From a bag of deer tallow, she added a yellow smear of grease and then, forcing Pinch to lie still, she spread the paste on his burns and propped him against a tree. She brought him lots of maple-flavored water, stroked his forehead carefully, soothingly. And as she did this, surprisingly enough, he stopped howling. He looked up at his big sister with a gaze of intense trust.

By the time Nokomis, Deydey, and the others returned, Pinch was quiet and looked alertly around, bright-eyed as Andeg, wondering what trick he could play next. Nokomis bent to her grandson's feet, looked carefully at what Omakayas had done.

"*Ho!* I couldn't have done a better job," she said, pleased. Nokomis gazed proudly at her granddaughter for several long moments. "My girl, you're strong in healing."

"And now," said Deydey kindly, touching his son's prickly hair, "what was that I heard you yell before the syrup spilled onto your feet? What about your first kill?"

Pinch looked at his father. He opened his mouth. He tried to tell about the deer, but somehow he just couldn't. He was amazed at himself for not lying.

"It was just a mistake," he mumbled at last, looking at his sister. "Megwetch," he said, embarrassed to be caught thanking her. It was just that his feet had hurt so badly, and then felt so much better! How had she done that?

So that was the very first time Omakayas made someone better with her medicine. Through the years, she would think back to that moment proudly, for her treatment worked. Pinch's feet were better in very little time. His pain was soon gone, and he had no puckered scars. It felt very good to her to heal another human, even if that human was Pinch.

CHAPTER THIRTEEN

One Horn's Protection

 "THIS WAS SUCH A good sugaring year," said Deydey, "we'll be able to pay off most of our bill at the trader."

"I want to come, I want to come," yelled Pinch. Deydey was loading his big pack frame with bound makuks of sugar. There was much, much more than they would use all year. Old Tallow had her fill of sugar, too, and Nokomis said that in all of her memory there had never been a sugar year like this one.

At the trader's, Deydey paid off the winter's debt and bought a length of blue broadcloth for Mama to sew into a dress. He bought Pinch some calico trim for a pair of makazins, and a piece of velvet cloth for Angeline to use as she wished. For Nokomis, sewing needles and a cup of shining copper. For Omakayas, he bought a small cross stamped out of German trade silver. The night Deydey gave her the cross, she sewed it onto the front of her dress. Andeg loved the look of it and tried constantly to pluck it from her dress—he landed on her shoulder over and over and nearly hung upside down to try and peck at it with his beak.

In the morning, Andeg greeted Omakayas with fluttering wings, ducking his head to accept a little scratch, cooing with a sweet and gurgling sound. Omakayas had never heard a crow make such a sound before, and she knew it was a special sign of affection. She was certain of it one day when Andeg hopped toward her with a twig in his beak. She carefully took it, thanked her crow, and laid the twig aside. All that day, wherever she turned, there was Andeg, hopeful, carrying a piece of bark for her. At last, Omakayas scratched Andeg's neck and sat down to feed him and talk to him. He listened, his lids closed, blue, his head tucked down in quiet bliss.

"You want to make a nest with me, don't you?" said Omakayas. "I can't. I love you, but I'm not a bird." She was surprised to find that, as she said this, tears formed in her eyes. Andeg loved her so much!

"You will have to find another crow," she said, very gently. Andeg didn't seem to hear. Still, after that he would leave for hours at a time. Now Omakayas was afraid that he would be taken for a wild bird and shot or killed. She attached a bit of red wool to his leg. Andeg managed to pull it off with his clever beak. He could untie almost anything if he worked hard enough.

One day, while Omakayas was working just outside the cabin in the cool air, watching a fire Nokomis had made to smoke some of the fish Deydey caught just at ice breakup, there was a sudden harsh cawing of crows. A group of wheeling, excited black birds passed overhead. Just like that, without a good-bye, Andeg jumped off her shoulder. He flew, zinging upward into the midst of the flock. In a second, he was indistinguishable from the others.

Omakayas felt her heart squeeze shut painfully as the birds passed out of sight. He was gone. Maybe she should have cut away essential feathers from his wings, but she couldn't stand to think of him a captive. No, she decided, though her heart hurt, it was better that he join with his own kind. He wasn't human, no matter how often he said "Gaygo, Pinch," or greeted her at the door, croaking out, "Ahneen, Ahneen!" Andeg stole and hoarded bits of bright cloth and shiny metal shards, he

wasn't a human, he was still a crow, and she couldn't change that.

She couldn't change that any more than she could change being who she was, Omakayas, who heard the voices of plants and went dizzy. Omakayas, who talked to bear boys and received their medicine. Omakayas, who missed her one brother and resented the other, who envied her sister. Omakayas, the Little Frog, whose first step was a hop. Omakayas who'd lost her friend.

She thought she had cried all the tears she had

to cry, but still found there were some left for Andeg. Omakayas put her hands to her face and sobbed until she felt just enough better. After all, she thought, Andeg was wild and she had always known it, always expected this moment to come. The thought comforted her. There in the yard, looking into the heart of the fire, Omakayas suddenly experienced a strange awareness. Like Andeg, she couldn't help being just who she was. Omakayas, in this skin, in this place, in this time. Nobody else. No matter what, she wouldn't ever be another person or really know the thoughts of anyone but her own self. She closed her eyes. For a moment, she felt as though she were falling from a great height, plunging through air and blackness, tumbling down with nothing to catch at. With a start of fear, she opened her eyes and felt herself gently touch down right where she was, in her own body, here.

CHAPTER FOURTEEN

Full Circle

ONCE AGAIN, THE FAMILY was building the birchbark house, moving out into the woods, dragging pots and other provisions out to the fishing camp where they would live. While she sewed mats together and reset the willow poles, Omakayas often experienced the haunting sense of things missing. She thought she'd forgotten something, or someone, then of course she remembered. Neewo and Ten Snow had left huge holes in her life, and Andeg a tiny one black as pitch and hoarse with laughter. Although spring, with all the force of its poised new growth, called to her, although the tender new buds, opening magically, touched her heart, there would always be a shadow to her laughter, a corner of sadness in her smile.

All day, Omakayas and her grandmother worked hard retying the intersections on last year's willow frame. Nokomis cut new bark, made fancy overlaps and rain diversion flaps. As soon as the house was finished, when there was no way left for him to help any way at all, Albert LaPautre came by for a visit. His round stomach had flattened out a trifle from the starvation winter, but he was by no means thin. He was excited. As usual, he'd had a vision, only this time he seemed to think that it was something very, very special. It was so amazing that he couldn't contain himself from blurting it all out at the fire, in everyone's presence.

"I have a new spirit helper," he declared, his voice portentous.

"Owah!" Father made an exaggerated sound of surprise and sat back, filling his pipe. Fishtail smiled in good humor, and made a gesture toward LaPautre that meant, "please, continue."

Puffing out his chest, raising his voice to an important pitch, Albert commenced his story.

"I admit to you that this occurred because of evil in my heart!"

"Oh, really," said Nokomis, her voice amused. "And *you* a man of such true virtue . . ."

"Yes, I know." LaPautre waved his hands modestly, as if to sweep away his incredible perfections.

Everyone then waited, expectant, for LaPautre to continue. Of course, having caught their interest, he puffed long in concentration to draw out the suspense.

"I was thinking about taking, well, actually *stealing*, one of Old Tallow's traps," said LaPautre. He put his hands up at the sounds of Mama's outrage. "Wait," he said to Mama, "hear me out."

She glared, but gave him the courtesy of her silence.

"She owes me a good trap!" protested LaPautre. "I gave her two skins once!"

"Two skinny muskrat skins," muttered Nokomis, but she hushed herself.

"So I went to her house when she was gone," said LaPautre, "to remove a trap from the lean-to where she keeps them. That's when it happened."

"What?" Pinch was breathless.

"Please be silent while I tell my story," LaPautre admonished. "It is powerful, I know, but you must respect my relationship with the winged ones and listen closely."

"Well, get on with it, we're listening," said Deydey, straining to keep the laughter from bursting out of his voice.

"Here is what happened!"

LaPautre made a final puff and drew himself up to his most solemn height. Unfortunately, whenever he pulled up his shoulders, his round belly popped out in a comical arc. Nevertheless, he went on. "I was approaching the house, I was putting out my hand, I was choosing the trap I would take . . ."

"Go on," said Nokomis, grim with protective fury for her friend Old Tallow.

"Anyway," said LaPautre, "I was about to close my fingers on the trap when I heard a voice."

Nobody really wanted to encourage LaPautre, but at last Angeline could not contain her curiosity.

"What did it say?"

"It said"—LaPautre leaned forward and fixed them all with his keenest, slightly cross-eyed stare—"'Gaygo.' In other words, the voice said *not to do what* I *was doing*. I opened my eyes. My friends, a crow was sitting there, its eyes black and shiny as lake stones. My friends, it spoke to me. 'Ahneen,' it said. 'Ahneen,' I answered. 'Gaygo,' it warned me again. Then flew off."

LaPautre sat back and folded his arms across his

chest. He waited for the sounds of amazement and the hushed tones of respect. He waited for the nods from Deydey and the serious expressions of wonder from Mama and Nokomis. Instead, after a moment of amazed delight, his entire audience burst into howls of laughter. Deydey was overcome with hilarity, and every time he tried to explain to LaPautre, he sank into helpless sobs and guffaws. Nokomis and Mama were holding each other and laughing so hard tears came down their cheeks. Angeline had turned away and was pounding the dirt. Pinch jumped up and down, yelling. Omakayas was laughing for another reason besides the coincidence, for Andeg was near, had survived, might come back someday!

LaPautre, slowly picking up his things, turned to the laughing family in a state of bewilderment. He put out his hands as though to ask, but then, when Deydey tried to blubber an explanation, only to collapse in fresh laughter, LaPautre swiped his hand through the air and scratched his head. This was definitely not the reaction he'd expected! As he walked away, he wondered whether the entire family had eaten some sort of strange medicine, taken leave of their senses perhaps? He stroked his chin. Yes, he'd sleep on it. Maybe his guardian bird, the crow, would return and speak to him again. Maybe he would have another vision, and somehow obtain an answer.

◄○►

Again it was time for the family to plant; Yellow Kettle chopped at the tough winter-packed earth of their family garden. While the others broke dirt clods and struggled with roots, picked stones and smoothed out rough rows to plant, Pinch pretended to help. He kicked at tiny weeds and smoothed circles in the dirt with his hands. He threw mud balls until Yellow Kettle gave her hoe to him and told him that if he stopped working just once she would take away all of his play warrior weapons. His lower lip stuck out. He grumped. As he dug into the earth he wished he was a grown man already with nothing of this sort to bother him. Still, he found himself occasionally dragging makuks of water over to splash on Omakayas's planted seeds. His sister even thanked him once, which made him so warm and shivery inside, that he had to run and shout, louder than ever, at nothing.

The pumpkin seeds wore little silver patches, like French medals, and Nokomis blessed them gently as she pushed them into the soft new earth. The corn seeds were chubby and yellow in Omakayas's fingers. Angeline had acquired, from Fishtail, some corn with red flecks in it and Mama put these seeds into the ground with a special blessing, curious to see what their growth would bring. The ground harbored the sunshine and spread warm beneath their feet. As she planted one hill after another Omakayas felt the calm and sweetness of the earth and tears burned. Where was Neewo? She missed him. When they had finished planting, as though summoned, rain sprinkled down in a mist. The shower deepened the calm of the woods, ticked through the new leaves, lightly wetted the seeds sheltered in the earth.

Suddenly, just as they were leaving the field, Andeg appeared, wheeling through the air, dive-bombing the family with his familiar *"crawwk, crawwk."* Andeg swooped near but refused to land with his usual sweep on Omakayas's shoulder.

"Come, come, ombay!" called Omakayas with a thrill of happiness.

Pinch, who never was still, never kept himself from excitement, acted differently. He stood motionless and waited right next to his sister. He seemed to know something that Omakayas, in her eagerness to hold her pet, couldn't grasp. Andeg had become half wild, afraid of humans. Omakayas's waves and anxious calls were frightening to him. Pinch, on the other hand, actually understood that the quieter he stood the more likely their old friend was to trust him. And sure enough, Andeg did land. Right on Pinch's head. Pinch's eyes rolled up. He tried to see Andeg. The bird hopped up and down uttering his greeting. *Craakacraakacraak!* Omakayas was hurt, but instantly, and this was the gesture that forever changed the nature of the friendship

between her and her little brother; Pinch gently edged next to his sister, and with a short hop her Andeg jumped onto Omakayas' shoulder.

In the old days, Pinch would have teased her and made her feel bad because her bird preferred him. Something had changed.

"Megwetch, little brother," said Omakayas, surprised to say the word.

Pinch didn't seem to hear, he ran off immediately, shouting his head off. Tears burned in Omakayas's eyes, for as soon as Andeg was on her shoulder he trusted her once more. He pecked at her silver cross, hopped onto her head, gazed at her with the old, curious, questing expression of bird intelligence. As they started back from the field, he rode on her shoulder. Tenderly, as they walked along, the bird plucked up a strand of hair that had fallen loose from Omakayas's braid, and then he tucked it behind her ear.

◄○►

Not long after, Old Tallow brought deer bones to share with Grandma. For a time, the two women sat by the outdoor fire. The air was cool and the fire burned high, stacked with dry wood. Nokomis baked the deer bones, cracked them, and used a special long carved spoon to scoop out the hot rich marrow. After a while, Nokomis went out to look for Pinch, and Tallow called Omakayas over to sit near the fire with her.

"Have some tea," she said. "I made it fresh."

Omakayas shook her head, suspicious. Tallow was behaving in too serious and friendly a manner. Since when did Old Tallow make tea? Since when did she act as though she had something important to say? Omakayas tried to slip back into the lodge. But the tough woman seized her hand and bent her fingers around the handle of the cup. She had something in mind in this visit, it was clear, but Omakayas decided that whatever it was, she didn't want to confront it. Ever since she'd had a taste of Old Tallow's justice, she'd been wary of the fierce woman, and now, stubborn, Omakayas waited. She felt something flare in her heart. She didn't like to be bossed around.

Unwillingly, Omakayas accepted a cup and took a sip.

"Good. While you're drinking this," said Old Tallow, her strong, ropey arms arranged on her knees, her big feet breaking from her makazins as usual, her hat pulled low and her fierce eyes flashing, "I'll tell you the story of Omakayas. Maybe that will help you get over your little brother."

Omakayas put the cup down, picked it up again at Tallow's abrupt gesture.

"All right! I'll drink it! What do you mean?"

Omakayas frowned. What was this, a plan to get her to forget all about Neewo? She wasn't interested. She was still sad and loyal to her tiny brother. What did Tallow understand? Bitterly, she spoke. "I know the story of Omakayas. It all happened in the winter. She has a beautiful friend, a favorite baby brother. They die. She is left to cry for them."

"Not that story."

"What other story do you know about me?"

She wanted to tell the old woman to let her be, to go off and hunt, her favorite occupation. But because Old Tallow was, after all, an elder, and because Mama had always insisted that Omakayas be polite as possible to her elders, Omakayas pretended to listen to the story.

"When you were very tiny," Old Tallow began.

"What do you mean, when I was very tiny?" Omakayas tried to be good, but irritation burst out of her. "Mama had me, not you, and she held me, fed me, dressed me, all of those things. What do you know? What more is there to say?"

Old Tallow drew a deep breath, her eyes almost crossed with fury, but she kept her temper,

"You don't have any excuse to be rude, no matter how sad you are. You can't treat me in this disrespectful way."

Omakayas felt her throat shut with shock and embarrassment. She wanted to cry. Why was she acting like this?

"Eyah, okay then, I'm sorry," she said, more softly. "What are you going to tell me?"

"Haven't you wondered," said Old Tallow, a bit testy with the difficult girl Omakayas had become, "hasn't it occurred to you to ask why you didn't get the chimooko-man's sickness?"

"*You* didn't get sick," said Omakayas, stubborn.

"I *never* get sick," said Tallow.

"Nokomis stayed well."

"Your grandma already had the smallpox."

Omakayas remembered the tiny whited pit in the skin of her grandmother's cheek, but was still surprised to hear that Nokomis, too, had suffered the disease. She pondered for a moment, and then could not hide her curiosity.

"What about me?" she demanded, abrupt as Old Tallow herself.

"You, too."

"Me, too, what?"

"Had the scratching disease."

A panicky feeling bubbled up inside Omakayas, and she wanted to laugh to drive the feeling off.

"I couldn't have!"

"You wouldn't remember exactly what happened. You were a baby."

"Then why didn't Mama have it? Why did Mama get sick, too, this time?"

"Because," said Old Tallow, "you weren't with your mama, then."

Omakayas wanted to stop talking now. She could feel it. There was something else, something coming toward her, something deeper and huger that she didn't want to know. She tried to stop herself from asking the next question, but her curiosity was too great. She felt her voice rise.

"Where was I?"

"A different island," said Old Tallow. Her voice was stern, but there was an ache in her look that Omakayas had never before seen. "An island called Spirit Island where everyone but you died of the itching sickness— you were the toughest one, the littlest one, and you survived them all."

Tallow smiled mirthlessly, grim. "Starvation nearly got you next, but I managed to cheat the old hungry skull. Fed you broth of rabbits. Brought you back with me. This was before you were two winters old, my girl, before you said words yet, before you can remember anything."

Omakayas's mind tried to grasp what she was hearing, her heart tumbled into darkness and she could not speak. Now the line was crossed. She had to know everything.

"Mama, Deydey, Nokomis?"

"They took you as their daughter, loved you as their daughter, you are a daughter to them, and a sister to your brother, and to Angeline."

"You? Why did you give me away?" blurted Omakayas.

Old Tallow glared away, into the distance.

"Count yourself lucky! What kind of life with an

old bear hunter like Tallow? Nobody has ever stayed with Old Tallow. She drives them off. Eyah!"

The two sat together for a long, long time, there at the fire with the darkness gathering above them and to all sides. Old Tallow made a move to leave, but Omakayas said, her voice strange and hollow and small, "Daga, please, don't go."

Inside, she knew that there was something still to ask. Something about the story, which seemed both unbelievable and perfectly understandable, all at once. But she couldn't put it into words. Tallow went on speaking.

"I know now the reason you were sent to Yellow Kettle, to the old woman, to your Deydey, your brothers," said Tallow. She rustled in the tatters of her dress, groped for her smoking pipe, then remembered she was out of tobacco and let her hands splay restlessly in her lap.

"You were sent here so you could save the others," she said. "Because you'd had the sickness, you were strong enough to nurse them through it. They did a good thing when they took you in, and you saved them for their good act. Now the circle that began when I found you is complete."

Omakayas knew the question she needed to ask. She took a deep breath, and asked it forthrightly.

"Found me? How did you find me? How did you

know I was there unless you were on that island? Unless you, too, survived the sickness?"

Now Old Tallow fell silent, and in her mulling Omakayas could tell there was some unwillingness, something she did not want to say. But she shrugged, eventually, and told it right out.

"There was a canoe of men, my husband, Hat, among them. They passed by Spirit Island. Saw the dead. Saw you."

"So it was they who brought me back?"

"No," said Tallow, simply.

"They saw me," said Omakayas, making sure, "but they didn't save me."

Old Tallow shook her head in the dusk. Then she shook herself all over, just like one of her dogs.

"Hiyn! My husband, Hat, was a fearful fool. I was going to put his things out the door, anyway. When he told me that he and the other men had seen you, and gone on! Leaving you!" Old Tallow's voice took fury. "I made him leave. 'Don't show me your face, ever!' I said to him. And then I took my canoe over to that island."

The wintery trees clacked their branches, ticking and moaning. The wind picked up often, at dusk, on the island. Omakayas could feel in her heart what it was like for that baby, for herself, all alone with the dead, with her mother, walking from those she loved as though walking stone to stone. Somehow, deep inside, she remembered.

"It was spring," she said softly. "Zeegwun."

"Owah!" said Old Tallow in surprise, peering closely at her. "You remember!"

"The birds," said Omakayas, "I remember the birds, the songs of the birds."

"Owah!" Tallow was excited. "I had forgotten, myself. There were birds on that island, singing so prettily, so loudly! Too small to eat. The little birds with white throats, those sweet spring cries. Eyah! My girl, you remember them."

"They kept me alive," said Omakayas, to herself, not quite understanding her own words. "I remember their song because their song was my comfort, my lullaby. They kept me alive."

◄○►

Omakayas woke to a piercing spring music. Morning, it was morning, and it was the very same song she remembered from that other island, so long ago. This morning, in a tree near the birchbark house, she heard the white-throated sparrows calling out to one another.

"Where are you going?" Angeline asked sleepily.

"Out," said Omakayas.

"Errhg," said Pinch as she stepped over him and out into the fresh dawn world.

The sun was just peeping over the water, its light winking and growing. All around her there sounded voices of hundreds of white-throated sparrows. In the mild air of spring they were singing cheerfully, sweetly, as though to keep her company on the first morning of her life that she, Omakayas, knew the truth of her past. She was the girl from Spirit Island. She lived in a birchbark house. This was the first day of the journey on which she would find out the truth of her future, who she was. Singing, singing, the little birds told her something more. Their delicate song surrounded her, running in waves though the leafless trees.

Omakayas walked toward the strongest center of their music, and then, on a patch of thawed grassy ground, she lay back in the sun, her head against the bark of a fallen log. The birds, the whole earth, the expectant woods seemed to wait for her to understand something. She didn't know what. It didn't matter. Drowsily, she whistled along with the tiny sparrows. *Ingah beebeebee. Ingahbeebeebee.* Those sweet, tiny, far-reaching notes were so brave. The little birds called out repeatedly in the cold dawn air, and all of a sudden

Omakayas heard something new in their voices.

She heard Neewo.

She heard her little brother as though he still existed in the world. She heard him tell her to cheer up and live. *I'm all right,* his voice was saying, *I'm in a peaceful place. You can depend on me. I'm always here to help you, my sister.* Omakayas tucked her hands behind her head, lay back, closed her eyes, and smiled as the song of the white-throated sparrow sank again and again through the air like a shining needle, and sewed up her broken heart.

AUTHOR'S NOTE ON THE OJIBWA LANGUAGE

Ojibwa was originally a spoken, not written, language, and for that reason spellings are often idiosyncratic. There are also many, many dialects of Ojibwa in use. I apologize to the reader of Ojibwa for any mistakes and refer those who would like to encounter the language in depth to A *Concise Dictionary of Minnesota Ojibwa*, edited by John D. Nichols and Earl Nyholm, to the *Oshkaabewis Native Journal*, ed. Anton Treuer, and to the curriculum developed by Dennis Jones at the University of Minnesota.

GLOSSARY AND PRONUNCIATION
GUIDE OF OJIBWA TERMS

adisokaan (ahd-zoh-kahn): a traditional story that often helps explain how to live as an Ojibwa

ahneen (ah-NEEN): a greeting, sometimes in the form of a question

Akeeng (ah-KEEN): the earth

amik (ah-MIK): beaver

anishaa (ah-NISH-ah): a complex word used to begin an Ojibwa prayer, connoting humility in the mysterious greatness of creation

Anishinabe (AH-nish-in-AH-bay): the original name for the Ojibwa or Chippewa people, a Native American group who originated in and live mainly in the northern North American woodlands. There are currently Ojibwa reservations in Michigan, Wisconsin, Minnesota, North Dakota, Ontario, Manitoba, Montana, and Saskatchewan.

Anishinabeg (AH-nish-in-AH-bayg): the plural form of Anishinabe

apitchi (ah-PITCH-ee): robin

asema (ah-SAY-mah): tobacco of the sort normally used for smoking; one of the four most sacred plants of the Ojibwa

ashaageshinh (ah-SHAH-geh-sheen): crayfish

Awausesee (ah-WUHS-suh-see): the catfish dodem, or clan, a group within the Ojibwa tribe. Other dodems include migizi (eagle), mahingan (wolf), mahng (loon), and mukwah (bear)

ayah (ah-YAH): yes

bekayaan (beh-KAH-yahn): be quiet

biboon (bih-BOON): winter

◄ 241 ►

booni (BOO-nee): leave it alone

boozhoo (boo-SHOE): an Ojibwa greeting invoking the great teacher of the Ojibwa, Nanabozho

Bwaanug (BWAHN-ug): the Dakota and Lakota people, another Native tribe, whose reservations spread across the Great Plains

chimookoman (chi-MOOK-oh-man): word meaning "big knife," used to describe white people or non-Indians

chimookomanug (chi-MOOK-oh-man-ug): the plural form of chimookoman

daga (dah-gah): please

dagwaging (dah-GWAG-ing): fall

Deydey (DAY-day): Daddy

gaween (gah-WEEN): no

gaween onjidah (gah-WEEN ohn-jee-dah): I don't mean to do this

gayay neen (guy-AY neen): me too

gaygo (GAY-go): exclamation meaning "stop that"

geget (GEH-geht): surely, or for emphasis, truly or really

geget chiwohningeyz (gay-GET chi-who-ning-ehz): phrase meaning "good job" or "you did well"

hiyn (high-n): exclamation of sympathy or chagrin, meaning "that's too bad"

howah (HOW-ah): a sound of approval

ishte (ISH-tay): exclamation meaning how good, nice, pleasant

kinnikinnick (KIHN-ih-kihn-ihk): type of smoking mixture made of the inner bark of dogwood or red willow, sometimes mixed with regular tobacco

makazins (MAH-kah-zinz): footwear usually made of tanned moosehide or deerskin, often trimmed with beads and/or fur